THE BURNT HILLS

Mister Dixon bought a herd of horses from a man named Alvarez down in New Mexico, and sent two riders to bring them back to Colorado. The riders were Jeff Forman and Heber Madden. The remuda was stolen from them — they were robbed, beaten, and shot at. They had every reason to give up. Instead, they went after the thieves knowing that, in the ensuing battle, they must struggle to save not only the horses but also their own lives.

Books by Les Lewellyn
in the Linford Western Library:

CIMARRON

LES LEWELLYN

THE BURNT HILLS

Complete and Unabridged

LINFORD
Leicester

First published in Great Britain in 1992 by
Robert Hale Limited
London

First Linford Edition
published 1997
by arrangement with
Robert Hale Limited
London

British Library CIP Data

Lewellyn, Les
    The burnt hills.—Large print ed.—
Linford western library
    1. Western stories
    2. Large type books
    I. Title
    823.9'14 [F]

    ISBN 0–7089–5090–6

Published by
F. A. Thorpe (Publishing) Ltd.
Anstey, Leicestershire

Set by Words & Graphics Ltd.
Anstey, Leicestershire
Printed and bound in Great Britain by
T. J. Press (Padstow) Ltd., Padstow, Cornwall

This book is printed on acid-free paper

1

Adelentado

HIS name was Fausto Molinero. His eyes and hair were black. He was not above average height and his complexion was fair.

Tiburcio told them in English that his last name meant miller, that his first name, which was Fausto, had something to do with the devil.

They accepted this without question and without showing either curiosity or particular concern. Not until Heber Madden ate, drained his cup, leaned against the up-ended saddle to rest his back, and methodically rolled a cigarette. After lighting up he looked across the little hot fire to ask a question. "Why would a mother name her son after the devil?"

Tiburcio was much older than he

appeared to be. He spread his hands before reaching for the tin cup of coffee, "*Quien es*? They name them after *Jésus*, the saints, even after animals. There is a horseman in the country named *Caballo* Allen." Tiburcio drank coffee and resumed his meal. "A *caballo* is a horse."

Tiburcio finished his meal, put the tin plate aside and gazed at the pair of blue-eyed men opposite him. He'd had occasion to know many *gringos*. Some he had liked, some he hadn't liked.

Tiburcio was either close to seventy or in his seventies, he was unsure which, and his philosophy which had evolved over the years was very simple. There were only two kinds of people in the world: Ones he liked, ones he did not like.

One of the husky men across the little fire turned to the other. "Don't seem a lot different," he said. "I knew a woman named Heather, a feller named Joseph."

Tiburcio's bronzed-shaded face split

2

into a grin. "Joseph is *José*. You see, we are more alike than we are different. There must be a hundred *José*'s in the Raton country." He thought of something and asked a question. "Where you come from up north, do they have towns named for animals?"

Heber Madden thought a moment then brightened. "There's a place in Wyoming named Buffalo."

His partner, nodded. "I grew up in Antelope, Colorado."

The old man's eyes twinkled. "That town you rode through up north is Raton. Which means a rat. There is another town southeast of Raton called Boca Raton."

Heber's partner asked what that meant and Tiburcio laughed. "It means mouth of a rat."

The larger, heavier and much younger man stared. Heber Madden sounded incredulous. "Mouth of a rat?"

Tiburcio's laughter lingered at the looks on their faces. He said, "Years ago

I took delivery of horses for the Mexican army. It was all *gringo* country. The town was called *Culebra*. Snake." Tiburcio shrugged thin shoulders. "I think we are mostly different because we are alike. We say much the same thing in different languages."

The two strangers liked the old man. He made being different seem not actually very different at all. But that was a snap judgment. They *were* different and the extent of that difference lay ahead.

Madden's partner, a bull-necked individual with blue eyes that shaded off to grey, asked the old man about the horses they had come down here for.

Tiburcio lighted a very dark little cigar that gave off a powerful aroma of burning weeds. "My *patrón* sent me to tell you — because I speak English — that they will be at *Cañon de Caballos* in two days. I will come for you then, otherwise you might not find the place." Tiburcio paused. "My

4

patrón would like to know about the money."

Jeff Forman's eyes were narrowed. "If *caballos* means horses. The way you say canyon is the same way we say it. So there's a place called Horse Canyon?"

Tiburcio's eyes twinkled. "You will pick up the language fast, friend. Yes; Horse Canyon."

Tiburcio arose, dusted his seat and considered the *norteamericanos*. "There is something I should tell you . . . Mexican rurales want those horses too."

Jeff raised both eyebrows. "*Rurales?*"

"They are Mexico's constabulary soldiers. On our side of the border we don't have anything like them. Up here we called them Red Flaggers because their banner is red, the colour of blood. They have the power of life and death. They are very dangerous men."

Jeff and Heber arose facing the older man. Jeff said, "We contracted for those horses."

Tiburcio nodded. "All I know is that their *capitan* came to the ranch three days ago. He wanted horses. My *patrón* told him he had agreed to sell the horses to an American up north who would send men to take delivery of them." Tiburcio's gaze wandered and returned. "The *Rurale* rode away without another word. My *patrón* said you should know."

Heber Madden let his breath out slowly. "You're sayin' these Mex soldiers may try to get our horses?"

Tiburcio looked straight at Heber Madden. "It can happen, friends. It has happened before. Many times."

"Messicans come over the border and take horses?"

"Yes. Especially if there is trouble down there."

"Is there trouble down there, Tiburcio?"

The old man shrugged. "Not now, no, but my *patrón* told me any time Rurales come up here for horses, there must be trouble coming." The old man made a wry smile. "It is springtime, friends . . . " He made a small gesture to indicate it was the time of year for such things to happen.

After the old *vaquero* left Jeff sat down again, looked into the fire and when Heber returned from looking after their horses, Jeff said, "We need to find the nearest army post."

Heber drained the little speckleware pot of coffee and sighed. "Mister Dixon said it would be a holiday." Heber drank before completing it. "We should have asked him if he'd ever been down here." As he flung away coffee grounds he also said, "It's up to the local law or the army to protect the interests of folks doin' business down here. In the morning we'd ought to ride into that little town. We need more grub anyway."

They bedded down with sober thoughts. Not only was the country different than what they were accustomed to but clearly so were the people . . . Mouth of a Rat, for Chris' sake!

7

The town of Adelentado was more nearly a village. It had a wide main roadway, other roads and paths leading among the outlying residences, and most of the buildings were made of mud. They had thick walls, sometimes three feet thick. There were several wooden structures, a general store, the smithy, and opposite that structure was the livery barn. It was about half wood, the other half was thick adobe. At one time it had been the headquarters of the Mexican *commandante*, but that had been quite a while ago. When Mexico still owned the Southwest.

The cafe was manned by a thick, heavy man named Millard Filmore Jones. Having been named for a US president did not appear to be something he cherished. Locally he was called Peca because he was freckled. His hair was orange red, what remained of it, and at one time he had been an impressive individual. Now, in middle age, he had run pretty much to fat.

When Jeff Forman ascertained that

the constable of Adelentado was out of town, the partners crossed to the cafe where the big freckled man eyed them with candid interest. Very few people passed through, and, having once been a rangeman over in Texas, Peca rustled their meals, filled cups with coffee, and settled hips against the pie table, folded massive arms over his chest and said, "You boys are a ways from home, aren't you?"

Jeff nodded. Heber went on eating. The big man tried once more to get a conversation going. "I used to work cattle."

Heber raised his head. "Up north?"

"No, in Texas, and for a while in In'ian Territory. You boys ever been over there?"

They hadn't. Heber was drinking coffee so Jeff answered, "Nope. We're from Wyoming, Colorado, and once over into Idaho."

Peca Jones considered that. "It's different down here. In some ways it ain't, but mostly it is."

9

Jeff studied the larger man. "How long you been down here?"

"About thirty years, I guess." Peca raised dark eyes with muddy whites to gaze past the window to the dusty roadway. "I don't know why. Gawd knows it ain't much of a town."

Heber pushed his empty plate aside to lean on the counter. "Do you know a feller named Tiburcio Something-or-other, who rides for a Messican stockman named Alvarez?"

Peca's muddy eyes moved down to Madden. "Alvarez, *amigo* is *Don* Esteben Alvarez. *Don* means mister. It's a sign of respect. The Alvarez ranch covers more land that you could ride over in two weeks . . . Messicans don't like bein' called just Alvarez. They don't like bein' called Mister Alvarez. Down here it's *Don*. It shows respect."

Heber tucked this additional scrap of information away and held up an empty cup as he said, "This feller Tiburcio works for *Don* Alvarez?"

Peca spoke while re-filling the cup. "Yeah. Tiburcio Reyes. I know him well. He's one of Don Alvarez's *mayordomos*. That's sort of like a foreman up north, or a rangeboss. He's been around since just about everyone in town can remember. What about him? You met him?"

They had indeed met Tiburcio, but he'd not told them his last name. Not that it mattered a hell of a lot. Jeff said, "Real savvy feller."

Peca agreed with that. "For a fact. He knows every yard of country for a hunnert miles in all directions. He's as good a roper and *reindador* as ever came down the road."

Peca looked at them. Their blank expressions told him what he had already guessed. "A *reindador* is a man who reins horses."

Jeff nodded, "A horse-breaker."

Peca rolled his eyes. "Mister, anyone can break a horse. A *reindador* is the feller who puts a rein on him. Until you've seen some of these fellers work their horses . . . Well, when you go back up north you'll never be the same."

Jeff was rolling a smoke when he asked the cafeman when he thought the constable would be back in town? Peca answered in a slightly different tone of voice. "He's got a hell of a lot of country to cover. There's always some damned fool gettin' into trouble. When you see the door of his *calaboza* open you'll know he's back." Peca narrowed his gaze. "Are you fellers lawmen from up north?"

Jeff shook his head. "No. We're down here to take delivery on some horses."

"From Don Alvarez?"

"Yeah," Heber said, arising to spill silver atop the counter. He and Jeff returned to the wide, not exactly attractive roadway unaware that Peca Jones had remained leaning against his pie table, arms folded, looking out at them.

The town left much to be desired

in comparison to what the northerners were accustomed to. Here, the main wide thoroughfare had residences among the places of business. People came and went, about half Mex, half gringo.

Jeff and Heber went down to the livery barn. It was not only cool in the wide, long runway, it was also gloomy. The man who watched them enter while leaning on a four-tined fork, was lanky, turkey-necked and shrewd eyed. He had been in Adelentado for eleven years. He had arrived there with a saddlebag full of money and looking over his shoulder. His name was Heck Durham. At least that's the only name he was known by in the area.

He asked if the northerners wanted their animals. They asked if Adelentado had a hotel. Heck Durham almost laughed. "There's a place behind the saloon where, if it ain't taken up or spoke for, the saloonman rents out."

A rider passed by. He and Heck exchanged a wave. On a hunch Jeff asked if that had been the local

13

lawman. It had. The partners left Heck, like Peca, gazing after them as they struck out for the jailhouse, an unprepossessing square building with walls three feet thick and two strap-steel cages off the lawman's office.

It was a little later than mid-afternoon, shadows were growing on the lower end of town.

2

A Language Difficulty

THE town marshal or constable was referred to simply as *Jefe* Fausto, or *Jefe* Molinero. Chief. It was understood what he was chief of: The law in Adelentado and its countryside.

He was a man of average height with fair skin and very black hair and eyes. He was a *Criollo*, a Mexican Creole, which simply meant that he was of Spanish descent, but had been born in Mexico, as such he was considered an impure Spaniard. The caste system was rigidly observed elsewhere, but not in such a far place as New Mexico Territory, which in any case no longer belonged to Old Mexico so therefore its caste system, like other social and political burdens did not apply.

Jefe Molinero listened to the northerners without any expression. He asked if they knew Don Alvarez. They told him they knew Don Alvarez's mayordomo, and he smiled. They would never learn much about the *jefe*, but one thing was obvious, while he spoke English with the barest of accents, he spoke it very well.

As for Rurales, he gestured with both hands. "Talk is cheap. Here especially where life does not have a rhythm, rather it is like a still lake. Rarely does anything cause ripples. Friends, if Rurales were coming after those horses . . . Well, it is thirty miles to the border, there are three towns smaller than Adelentado between here and there. Over the years we have perfected a warning system. You can be easy, if they are coming we will know about it."

Heber was interested in Rurales. He told the *jefe* what Tiburcio had said. Molinero nodded politely. "He told you about how they work and who they are. They are the most feared and deadly of all Mexican armed units. As Tiburcio said, they are a law unto themselves. They can appropriate, execute, they can even cross the border, something I cannot do nor can our army cross into Mexico. But they have the authority of the Mexican government to cross in pursuit of criminals, *pronunciados*, which are rebels, revolutionaries." Molinero offered coffee which Madden and Forman declined. As they arose to depart Heber told the lawman they would take delivery of the horses in another day or two at a place called Horse Canyon, and be on their way.

Fausto Molinero saw them to the door. As they strolled in the direction of the general store to get provisions he leaned in his doorway watching.

The weather was favourable to just about all human activity. The sky was flawless blue, the days were pleasantly warm, and northeasterly where a dense stand of dead trees stood, called by the natives Burnt Timber, there was inviting shade.

Jeff and Heber struck camp and rode over the countryside. They found what they were certain was the Alvarez ranch. It was the only really large livestock operation they had come across. They sat in front of their horses on a thick topout and studied the place.

The buildings, of which there were many more than a man saw on northerly ranches, seemed to house riders with families. There were children darting among them, and lasso-rope clotheslines. There were also women.

South of the outbuildings was the main-house, long, low with red tiles on the roof and a thick wall completely surrounding it. Jeff thought that wall was for protection although in most places it was no more than waist high. Where it was higher appeared to be an area of some size behind which was the front doorway.

They spent the next day scouting for Horse Canyon. It was not much of a chore. There was dust farther out where riders were bringing horses in.

They found another point of vantage and watched. There appeared to be about eight or ten vaqueros bringing in the horses, they consistently lost cut-backs and made no attempt to go after them. Heber dryly remarked that as many animals as they were driving into the canyon, they could afford to lose some.

By evening they were back at their original camp site, horses hobbled in good grass, the sun turning bronze as it descended, eating a decent meal of tinned meat, peas and spuds. They also had more coffee.

Heber was of the opinion Tiburcio would be along either tonight or tomorrow. Keeping as large a remuda as had been driven into that canyon could only be temporary. The walls of Horse Canyon as well as the southern end were nearly perpendicular bluffs. Goats would have been unable to escape except by the way they had entered. It did not need mentioning that since there would be only one way back out of the canyon, riders would be out there with bedrolls and food to be certain the horses did not escape.

Grass in a place like that canyon could not support an over-stock more than a day or two. And if there was no water in there . . . Jeff grinned. "When we turn 'em north they'll head for a spring. We'll only have to keep 'em in sight until they're heavy with water and run-down."

Heber scrubbed his tin plate clean with swatch of grass, sucked his teeth as he moulded a smoke and lit it before mentioning what had been bothering him since Harold Dixon, their employer, had sent them south.

"I'll be relieved to hell and back when I hand the money in my belt to this feller Alvarez."

Jeff was settling comfortably against his up-ended saddle when he commented on that. "I reckon. But tomorrow or the next day you'll have the bill of sale an' he'll have the money."

Heber pensively smoked before speaking again. "As long as it was only you'n me, I didn't worry much, but you remember Tiburcio asking about the money?"

"Yeah. I also noticed you changed the subject."

"Well, if the old Mex knows, an' the town constable or whatever they call 'em down here, knows, that sort of increases the odds against only you'n me and Alvarez knowing."

Jeff re-settled his back-rest. He and Heber Madden had partnered other times since hiring on with the Dixon outfit three years earlier. Heber was conscientious or he wouldn't be Mister Dixon's top hand, but he was a worrier and always had been, at least since Jeff Forman had known him. As he got more comfortable against his back-rest he considered the sober expression of Heber and said, "What the hell, Heber, we covered a lot of miles, passed through some pretty bad country, an — "

"An' we looked like any other pair of riders on old saddles wearin' faded shirts and pants. No bushwhacker in his right mind would have stopped us. But this is different; folks know why we're down here, an' it wouldn't take much sense to know Alvarez don't *give* his horses away."

After a moment when both men were silent Heber said something else that had troubled him since accepting the money-belt from Mister Dixon. "Why'n hell didn't he just make one of them bank drafts?"

Jeff had the answer off the top of his head. He had no idea it might be right. "Because maybe they don't do business down here with bank drafts. I've seen more Messican money down here than our money."

Heber killed his smoke, studied the sky, the position of the moon and grunted that he was going to turn in.

He never made it. Neither did Jeff Forman.

Out of nowhere a voice calmly said, "*Buenas noches, vaqueros.*"

As Madden and Forman straightened around the same voice said, "*No pistoles, Señores. Descanso, Señores. Be tranquilo. Dinero, por favour. Andale Dinero hombre!*"

Whatever those last three words meant, there was no mistaking their menace.

Jeff replied, "We don't know what the hell you are talking about."

For several seconds there was silence. To Jeff and Heber it seemed that what Jeff had said made no more sense to the man they couldn't see than what he had said to them.

One thing was a lead pipe cinch, whoever he was, out there, he was not friendly. Heber scarcely breathed. Sure as hell this was to be a robbery. He would have cursed the Adelentado lawman and Tiburcio if he'd had the time.

Two Mexicans came out of the darkness with cocked sixguns held low. One was very dark and pock-marked, the other one was not as dark but had a wound of a mouth and venomous black eyes. They looked dirty, sweat-stained and willing to kill the men sitting on the ground.

A third man came forward. He was not tall. He looked as dangerous as the murderous-eyed man and was almost as fair complexioned. He spoke quietly. "The money," he said in accented English. "Or we kill you."

Heber's shellbelt and holstered sixgun had been removed before he climbed into his blankets. Jeff scarcely breathed. If Heber even looked like he was going to resist all hell was going to bust loose, and gawd only knew how many more were out yonder in the night.

It was a bad place to die, in the middle of nowhere among people they did not understand. Jeff quietly said, "Give it to him, Heber."

The third Mexican to walk up smiled

slightly. He clearly understood English, at least some English. "You will live," he said, and paused to frame more words in an unfamiliar tongue. He shrugged. "*Morir*," he said turning to the taller man with the slit of a mouth and the black, murderous stare.

Jeff spoke quickly, "It's under his shirt in a belt."

The Mexicans looked from Jeff to Heber. For a moment Jeff thought they would be killed; it seemed that Mexican who knew some English was making sense out of what Jeff had said.

Heber snarled, "What are you trying to do? They — "

Jeff snapped back. "You're goin' to get us both killed. What the hell good are we to Mister Dixon or anyone else if we're dead?"

The light-complexioned Mexican spoke shortly to the other two. They sprang forward catching Heber as he was desperately trying to stand up. Their combined weight carried him to the ground on his back. They pinned his arms.

The other man came forward holstering his sixgun and drawing a wicked-bladed knife from somewhere under his coat. He made two slashes. The first one cut Heber's shirt, the second one slashed his trousers at the waist. The money-belt was exposed.

Heber arched and strained. He tried to kick. The man trying to tug the money-belt loose lost patience. He reversed the knife and struck Heber on the head with the weighted handle. That ended the struggle.

They got the money-belt, two of them started back out into darkness but the third Mexican lingered a moment before sheathing his knife and smiled at Jeff. "You keept him alive. *Adios.*"

Jeff heard them leaving. For a fact there had been a band of them, not just those three. He went over and knelt where blood was running down Heber's face. The gash was deep, Heber was unconscious. Jeff made a crude bandage from two bandannas which slowed the flow but did not stop it.

He sat back on his haunches. He did not want to leave Heber but if ever a man needed care it was his partner.

He considered tying Heber on his horse and leading the animal over to Adelentado, but abandoned that notion because he doubted if there was a doctor over there, also because the jarring ride would probably keep the blood flowing.

It was about a three mile ride to the Alvarez ranch. That was a couple of miles closer than Adelentado.

He brought in both horses, re-bandaged the torn scalp using both arms out of his only spare shirt, strained to get Heber astride, tied him, mounted his own animal and struck out.

It turned cold before he caught a scent of wood smoke. He could not ride out of a walk. Before that smoke-fragrance had increased much some dogs barked in the distance. He set his course by their racket, reached the yard with a streak of sickly grey along the eastern turn of the world, rode directly to the barn, stiffly dismounted and got Heber down. Madden groaned and opened his eyes. Jeff said, "Lean on me."

His partner made a completely irrelevant remark. "I got to pee."

Jeff turned back just past the barn opening and said, "Go ahead."

Heber was unsteady on his feet, he weaved and wobbled. Jeff stood close to catch him if he fell, but he completed his chore without falling, by which time those yammering dogs had roused half the ranch. There were lighted candles among the outbuildings.

Tiburcio appeared with a shotgun. He stopped, scowled, muttered something and got on Heber's far side as they began crossing in the direction of the main-house where a more brilliant variety of light showed.

Don Alvarez met them at the door holding a long-barrelled pistol. He had a maroon dressing gown over his *pajames*. He was dark but with fair skin. Right at this moment his hair stood in all directions and his face was puffy from sleep.

He did not speak as Tiburcio and Jeff got Heber inside. They laid him flat out on the floor. Don Alvarez disappeared, they could hear him giving orders in rapid-fire Spanish. When he returned two thick, dark women appeared bundled in heavy robes. They shouldered the vaquero and Forman aside. Don Alvarez took them aside. For a moment there was a swift exchange between Tiburcio and his *patrón* before Don Alvarez turned to Jeff, using slightly accented English he asked what had happened.

After Jeff explained *el patrón* turned to watch the women. They washed Heber and made a fresh, more professional bandage. They then hoisted him between them and later, Jeff would remember how easily they had handled his weight.

They disappeared toward the rear of

the house. Don Alvarez sighed, ran bent fingers through his hair and asked Jeff to describe their attackers, which Jeff did.

Don Alvarez and Tiburcio exchanged a look. The older man shrugged, said something in Spanish and stood in silence for his *patrón* to respond.

He did. Jeff saw a side of the man he had not seen before. Don Alvarez's dark eyes flashed, his profanity was fierce; it required no knowledge of Spanish to guess about what he was saying. When he had vented his fury he asked Jeff if the men had gotten the money.

Jeff nodded, described how Heber had defied them, had had his scalp split for the effort, and found a chair to sit down.

Don Alvarez addressed his vaquero again, in sharp, clear sentences. Tiburcio nodded, went as far as the door before turning back. He asked about Jeff. *El patrón* told him to go without him, he wanted more conversation with the *norteamericano.*

Tiburcio departed. Don Alvarez raised his voice. When one of those sturdy, dark women appeared, he told her in Spanish their guest needed breakfast. The woman listened impassively and disappeared.

Don Alvarez went to a beautifully hand carved small case, opened it, filled two glasses with dark wine, handed Jeff one and retained one. He was calmer now as he sank into a chair.

He made half a salute with his glass, sipped wine and lowered the glass as he spoke. "Now what happens? The horses are in the canyon."

Jeff did not raise the glass as he considered the stocky, older man. "How long can you hold them?" he asked.

"Two days, no more than three days then the feed will be eaten down."

Jeff finally tasted the wine. It was neither sweet nor bitter. Under different circumstances he would have enjoyed it.

"You know the country," he told the older man. "You know the people. Who would they have been? I'll tell you one thing, there were more of them than just those three. When they left it sounded like maybe as many as six or eight horses."

Don Alvarez got more comfortable in the chair. The shock had passed, now back to business. "There are always outlaws, sometimes two or three, sometimes parties of them. This has always been a lawless country, friend. I sent Tiburcio to look at their tracks. He was to take other riders with him. I told him if he found those men to come back. I would pay him twice his wages for the month." Don Alvarez made a thin smile. "If anyone can track them Tiburcio can. He was tracking men — and Indians — when I was a baby. My father told me when I was older that if anything happened to Tiburcio, he could not be replaced."

One of those blocky, flat-faced dark women appeared. She waited until Don

Alvarez noticed her then told him in Spanish a meal was ready.

Dawn had arrived but in the nearly windowless hacienda of the family Alvarez y Pacheco, it could still have been dark because there were candles. There were also coal oil lamps but they were rarely used.

3

The Same Ends, Different Means

JEFF was in a dark, windowless bedroom whose furnishings were sparse but massive when he and Heber heard men talking in the front of the house.

Heber's wound was swollen but whatever powder the *mestizo* women had put on it had stopped the bleeding. If he had known the powder was crushed spider webs he would have felt less agreeable toward their talents.

He had a bad headache, so bad in fact his eyes watered, but he was fully conscious, aware of what had happened right up until he was knocked senseless, and he was furious. He was venting his feelings about this part of New Mexico, the people who inhabited it, and those thieves when Don Alvarez entered the

34

room. Now, he had shaved, his hair was combed, his attire, while different to the gringos, looked serviceable. For example, there was some kind of soft leather sewed on the inside of each leg, it went up in the back where a man's rear would fit a saddle.

He was polite, which was one thing the pair of *norteamericanos* would learn. Don Alvarez was always polite, except when he was angry, then he was merciless.

Tiburcio, he told them, had tracked the *bandidos*. They had ridden fifteen miles before making their camp. Don Alvarez was going after them with his riders.

Jeff mentioned Fausto Molinero and the patrón showed a scornful small smile. "Here, on my land," he told them. "I am the law." He asked if Jeff cared to ride with him.

Jeff was tired, but he had been fed. He nodded, winked at his bed-ridden partner and accompanied the older man.

Outside, the sun was already high. Ordinarily this time of year, late springtime, the day would have been hot, but there was a veil-like high overcast which allowed sunlight to reach through but which blunted most of its heat.

Someone had put Jeff's outfit on a muscled-up chestnut horse. The vaqueros still rode Mexican saddles, called *esillo vaqueros*. They had a fork but no swells. They also had what seemed to Jeff to be a ridiculously large saddle horn. He noticed something else. Most of the stirrups were steel, a few were engraved. Some of the riders had the traditional wooden stirrups.

As he mounted the chestnut he thought that no one in their right mind would ride steel stirrups.

There were five riders, seven counting the patrón and Tiburcio, who had already ridden close to thirty miles and by all rights should have been tired. He sat his fresh horse as though he too was fresh.

Don Alvarez led with Tiburcio close behind, and at times riding beside Don Alvarez.

It was a long ride. Normally to cover that distance would require half a day, but the New Mexicans alternated between short walks and miles of slow-loping. They were in the vicinity where Tiburcio had tracked the thieves with the sun well off-centre but still high.

It was timbered country. There had been a fierce fire here, but it must have been some years back because there was fairly tall second growth. It was a fairly large area. The natives called it 'fuego arbolada' which, roughly, meant 'burnt timber'.

The land was hilly with stretches of woodland running for miles. Below was grassland, also uneven and veined with erosion gullies.

To Jeff it was somewhat reminiscent of the country he came from where there were also areas of burned trees. The difference in New Mexico, at least this part of it, was that as far as he could determine there was neither wild animals or livestock.

Tiburcio dismounted to tie his horse. The others took their cue from him. He and Don Alvarez unshipped carbines. Jeff followed that example.

Tiburcio led off through the mostly dead timber to a jutting place where there was no second growth. Here, they crept slowly.

Tiburcio stopped between two blackened dead trees, straightened up and swore in Spanish. Below, less than three or four hundred yards where a piddling creek ran, there was cold ash and cropped grass where riders had been.

He and Don Alvarez conferred while the others including Jeff rested. There was a little conversation among the vaqueros but not much. One vaquero, a buck-toothed wiry wisp of a man grinned and tried his English on Jeff. "Too *mucho* subbitches *bandidos*, no?"

Jeff nodded, smiled and let the discussion die.

Tiburcio rode down the slope in plain sight, scouted where the camp had been and flagged with his hat. He had the trail again.

This time they could not hasten, the ground was too rugged, forested with dead and living trees, and rocky. But old Tiburcio made as much haste as he dared.

The sun was lowering, shadows were forming, still pale but not for long. Tiburcio crested another of those topouts, dismounted and had his back to the others for a long time, until his patrón rode up and swung off too. Jeff watched them gesturing and talking. They seemed to be guessing which way the renegades had gone according to the route of least resistance for horsemen.

The wiry buck-toothed Mexican sidled up to Jeff and said, "It is a very nice day, no?"

He had said it loudly enough for his friends farther back to be impressed. Jeff agreed that indeed it was a very nice day.

The dark elf of a man then spoke again, this time gesturing upwards towards a sky free of clouds. "*Esta yo viendo* on me with you, no?"

Jeff looked up, looked down and nodded his head.

Tiburcio was back astride. He left the others skirting around a lip of land which fell away easterly. Don Alvarez stood alone watching. When his top hand was no longer in sight among the burned trees, he beckoned to Jeff. "He is going to find a high place where we can see their eating fire."

Jeff nodded about that, and wondered how much farther ahead the outlaws might be. He was not enthusiastic about riding in darkness through standing trees that were also black.

The sun was close to some distant timbered rims when Tiburcio appeared some distance away. He stood in his stirrups and waved his hat. Don Alvarez gave an order and swung up. He used the same route Tiburcio had used to get around that easterly barranca.

When they met the old vaquero he grinned at Don Alvarez and Jeff. "Two, maybe three miles. Their horses are hobbled."

Don Alvarez nodded and gestured. Tiburcio turned to lead the way.

Jeff considered the position of the sun. If they had to ride any distance it would be dusk or later when they got where Tiburcio was leading them. He was grimly satisfied at the prospect of getting the money back, but unsure of what lay ahead. There were seven of them. The men they were after had about the same number. That annoying dark scarecrow rode close and leaned as he grinned from ear to ear. "Now for us *muy matador*, no — partner?"

Jeff said, "*Matador?*" His companion slowly drew a stiff finger across his throat, still grinning.

Jeff nodded, looked ahead and said, "Yeah," but he was worrying about fading light again and Tiburcio showed no sign of halting.

Once, six or seven years back, Jeff

41

Forman had been dragooned while in town to ride with a posse after a man who had stolen a judge's thoroughbred horse. They had ridden themselves ragged and although there had been good sign to follow, they had never even gotten a sighting.

That was the extent of Jeff's manhunting and right now when he looked at the men he was riding with, he had a feeling that his education was about to be added to.

He was correct but he never would have imagined *how* it was going to be added to. For all of old Tiburcio's tolerant philosophy about differences being the same, New Mexico was neither Colorado nor Wyoming.

Dusk arrived, Tiburcio left them again, returned and smiled at Don Alvarez. Those two dismounted, conversed briefly, then led off afoot among the burnt timber, the scraggly second growth and now, thorny underbrush. The hike was uphill all the way, but gradually so.

Where Tiburcio halted the others stood in silence. Below and perhaps half a mile ahead where the ground was nearly level, there was a flourishing tongue of flame. It made shadows of seated men.

Tiburcio smiled at Jeff as he spoke. "Smart bandits would not have stopped even to eat."

It was getting darker by the minute as the riders followed Tiburcio on a rocky down-slope. The old vaquero never once dislodged a rock. The others were very careful, but that wiry gnome who was probably almost as old as Tiburcio, stumbled, which set up a miniature rock slide. On a still night sound carried. Another vaquero threw himself down atop the rocks.

Everyone held their breath. Down below a man arose, looked back and upwards, then sauntered away from the fire northward to pee on a large rock.

Don Alvarez bared his teeth at the wiry man, who seemed to wilt into himself. The quick-witted vaquero

43

arose, dusted himself off, passed the wiry man, called him a name and resumed his place among the others.

Down below the man who had walked toward the big rock sauntered back, took his place in the circle, and what could have been a genuine disaster for the stalkers, passed.

Tiburcio resumed the stalk, stopping occasionally to look back. The wiry gnome whose hide was the colour of wet mud, managed always to be glaring fiercely in the direction of that fire when Tiburcio stopped.

When darkness settled Tiburcio took an endless amount of time skirting the high place and finding a game trail downward. The trail, at least, was practically bare of rocks and had a thick layer of dust. Here, they could hike downward with slight chance of discovery.

On the lower grassland, un-even though it was, they could make better time. Right up to the moment a hobbled horse whinnied.

The renegades came up to their feet almost as one man. Tiburcio hissed and dropped flat. There was a low roll of heightened land ahead of them.

They scarcely breathed as voices came to them. Jeff, who understood nothing that was being said by the men around their fire, watched Tiburcio and Don Alvarez. They appeared tense but not fearful. One voice abruptly cut across the other voices. Jeff understood every word this time, and there was no accent. *That* one was a gringo.

He said, "Horses been rested enough. I don't feel easy. We better ride."

Someone grumbled in heavily accented English. "There is no way . . . Even if they used tracks they couldn't get this far."

The gringo replied in scrambled Spanish. "Look you; that was much money. Catching us you know what they will do!"

One of the Mexicans laughed but the others were upset, not nervous yet, but worried.

Tiburcio led off again, over the landswell, down its far side and up the next gentle slope. As he eased belly-down Don Alvarez dropped down beside him. Jeff raised his head. He could not see down the far side of their swell but he could see the fire and it was much closer. Within saddlegun range.

Tiburcio twisted to look back. The vaqueros were in an un-even line. Every man including Jeff Forman, had a saddlegun pushed forward. Tiburcio made a short chopping motion for the others to crawl up the slope where they could see.

At the fire someone said in Spanish his companions were imagining things, and sat back down. This man's action seemed reassuring. The others also sank back to the ground, only a rawboned man whose hair showed below the brim of his hat, remained standing. He glared at them. Jeff had a good view of that one as he crawled to the lip of the little rise, and *that* one was not a Mexican.

Tiburcio leaned to whisper. Don

Alvarez nodded. They shoved their Winchesters forward, dropped faces close to snugged-back stocks and when Jeff expected them to call to the men at the fire to throw their weapons away, both of them opened fire.

The standing man went over backwards, coat flapping. A Mexican whose back was to the landswell, threw up his hands and fell forward almost into the fire.

The vaqueros were firing at figures which had abruptly sprang up to flee. Jeff did not fire. He might have but it was over before he could pick a target.

It was over in less than a minute. Echoes chased one another against the hillsides but the firing was finished.

Tiburcio, who the others watched, did not stand up. Somewhere ahead beyond the fire a man was groaning. As long as that sound lasted Tiburcio remained where he was lying.

Jeff arose to one knee, the fire had been scattered but it still burned. Jeff thought he could count four dead men. When that moaning man no longer made a sound, he added him to the tally. He had thought there had been as many as six or eight. At the fire he had counted six. Five killed meant at least one was loose.

Tiburcio arose finally and moved ahead with his carbine left behind, his handgun cocked and ready.

Don Alvarez remained in the grass until Tiburcio had toed one corpse over onto its back, then he arose and went unerringly to the face-up gringo with the shaggy ash-coloured mane.

The silence was complete as they went among the dead. Tiburcio told the wiry, very dark man to go through their pockets, put everything in their hats. As this was being done a vaquero leaned above a body whose eyes stared back at him. Jeff was close by and saw the vaquero raise his sixgun before cocking it. Jeff hit the man with his shoulder, knocking him to the ground. As the vaquero got to his feet he bared his teeth. He would have raised the sixgun but Jeff already had his weapon belt-buckle high and cocked. They stood facing one another until Don Alvarez approached, said something and the vaquero walked away.

Don Alvarez regarded Jeff thoughtfully before speaking. "This one will die. Look at him. He had a bullet through his body high up. He is filling with blood from the inside. It would be an act of mercy . . . "

The dying Mexican spoke in a clear voice. "Patrón," he said bitterly and added more, all of it spoken with unmistakable hatred.

Jeff understood none of it. Don Alvarez gripped the gun in his fist but did not raise it. His answer to the Mexican was in Spanish. "May you rot in hell forever."

The dying man convulsed, blood flooded from his mouth. He died.

Tiburcio sent men to bring in the horses. He had counted the saddles. There were six, one with a small horn, swells and completely leather covered. A gringo saddle.

While the horses were being brought in Tiburcio studied the area. The escaping renegade could have gone in any one of three directions. Tiburcio had the strange horses saddled. He sent one man for their own animals and took the others in a wide-fanning hunt for the man on foot. He had not asked Jeff to go. He and Don Alvarez went among the up-ended hats.

All the money was not there although clearly it had been divided. Jeff went to the dead gringo, tore his clothing until he came to the moneybelt, and returned to hand it to the patrón.

Alvarez counted by dying firelight, re-counted then stood up with a small smile. "Mostly, it is here. The one Tiburcio will find will have the rest of it." Don Alvarez put his head slightly to one side and considered Jeff.

"I spent nine years north of the border, going to school. I know . . . the difference is that you hang them and we shoot them."

Jeff frowned. "Hell, he was dying. A man's got the right to die at peace."

Don Alvarez did not argue, he simply said, "Yes. At peace. A rope you tie around his neck, torture him while his sentence is read, while the priest prays . . . Here, one bullet, one second. *Sabe, amigo?*"

Jeff did not answer. He was looking far out where a sound of horsemen was clear. Don Alvarez also turned. "They found him," he said dispassionately, and walked forward.

Jeff's education continued as pink light outlined the easterly hills. The riders halted when their patrón reached them, sat like carved stone while Don Alvarez had a short conversation with the captured renegade, a nondescript, rumpled man of indeterminate age.

Jeff heard the words '*ley fuga*', mentioned several times. Within a short while he learned what they meant.

The renegade was freed of the rope

around his wrists. He stood a moment looking in all directions, then flung southward in a furious run. Nothing happened for some time, then the vaqueros dismounted, took aim and fired.

The fleeing outlaw was hurled ahead and rolled.

Jeff was scarcely breathing. Don Alvarez walked back shedding spent casings from his handgun and plugging in fresh ones. He stopped and spoke without looking up. "You don't give the condemned a chance — we do. If he could reach the rocks just short of where he died, he would go free."

4

Heading North

THEY fed the fire to have enough light to saddle and bridle the horses of the dead men. With Tiburcio leading again they went back up the trail to the burnt timber and rode at a walk in the southerly direction they had taken to reach that killing ground.

That wiry little dark man seemed always to be close when Jeff looked around. The ride back seemed to take more time than the ride out had taken. Tiburcio and the patrón rode ahead in a satisfied silence. After daylight arrived Jeff asked the gnome at his side if they shouldn't have buried the dead bandits. It took a little time for the vaquero to understand. He looked upwards where large dark birds were drifting in, some farther back and circling, others flying toward those circling birds. He grinned from ear to ear and said, "*Sopilotes*."

The led-horses offered no trouble, they had been ridden hard, if there had been any fractiousness in them before that hard ride, there was none in them now.

The sun was again slanting away when they reached the yard. Old men, women and children appeared in doorways to watch. The vaqueros ignored them until the horses had been cared for, then headed for their sturdy adobe *chozos*. They were tired and hungry men.

Don Alvarez took Jeff to the main-house where they parted. Jeff went to Heber's room and found his partner dressed and sitting in a chair. He told Heber what had happened. For a moment Heber said nothing, then asked if the money had been recovered. It had. He then said, "It's their country, Jeff."

There was no argument there. Jeff

wondered how long it would be before Heber could ride and the answer surprised him. "Tomorrow. The headache's gone. I'll have to wear my hat sort of high. Those In'ian women are good at patching folks up."

Don Alvarez appeared in the doorway to say a meal had been prepared. His expression was almost impersonal as he led the way. The diningroom was large with that same kind of massive, dark and very old heavy furniture. The same pair of expressionless heavy-set dark women served them.

The meal was excellent, at least Jeff thought so although he might have enjoyed it less if he'd known what some of the dishes consisted of. Goat meat, for example, and a savoury sauce of pounded berries and eggs with a faint taste of peppers.

Don Alvarez led them to the parlour, had them seated and got down to business. He had all the money, the horses now belonged to Mister Dixon and, as he had mentioned before, they could not be kept in the box canyon for more than another day.

Heber was willing to move them the next day. Don Alvarez smiled. "If you aim them north they will go willingly because they will be hungry and thirsty. If they go in the right direction all you will have to do is keep them in sight."

Outside in the dying day, Heber asked Jeff if he had recognised the man who had struck him among the dead thieves. Jeff had not thought of that. Now he did, and he shook his head.

He was dog-tired. Heber left him in the barn where he found hay to sleep in, went among the little earthen houses to talk with the vaqueros, heard Tiburcio's account of what had happened, ate with the old vaquero whose wife was equally as old and spry, then also bedded down in the barn.

His head-wound was swollen but the actual gash had scabbed over. There would always be a scar but if he lived to be old, when a man's hair got thin, only then would the scar be noticeable.

Jeff awakened ahead of sunrise, jostled Heber. They got dressed and were going after their horses when Tiburcio appeared in the pre-dawn gloom to take them to his *chozo* for breakfast.

Afterwards the old vaquero and two other men rode to the canyon with Jeff and Heber where two nighthawks sat near the canyon's mouth wrapped in blankets, Tiburcio told Jeff and Heber how it was done. He and his two riders would ease into the canyon, very carefully and quietly pick their way all the way to the rear barranca, then they would yell and use their riatas to spook the horses forward out of the canyon. He suggested that Jeff get on one side, Heber on the other side so the remuda would not scatter too soon, then led his two companions into the canyon.

It was still dark enough for them to work their way slowly toward the far end of Horse Canyon.

Heber and Jeff got into position. Dawn was coming, it was cold, the pair of nighthawks in their blankets also stood to one side ready to wave the blankets at any animal who tried to veer east or west.

When pandemonium broke loose far back, the horses panicked. The leaders came out of the canyon in a dead run. None offered to swing away but the men with blankets were ready if they tried. For the waiting gringos the signal to ride was the shouting of the vaqueros bringing up the rear.

They timed it very well. Tiburcio and his men halted to watch. Jeff swung in the saddle to wave. The Mexicans waved back.

For a solid hour what Don Alvarez had predicted proved correct. Jeff and Heber could not keep up with the running remuda, but they were able to cut back a few horses who, now and then, tried to break away and cut back.

It seemed to Jeff to require half the time to reach the burnt timber country this time as it had taken the other time. What caused problems was the standing dead trees, the rermuda was tiring, horses had to widen their course to avoid trees, but when they came to that trail above the barranca where the fight had taken place, they had no choice but to continue north although their gait ultimately slackened to a walk.

Jeff had no chance to show his partner where the fight had been, he was too far west to even shout. Not that it mattered now that they were on their way with the Alvarez horses, which were now the Dixon Ranch remuda.

They had a long drive ahead of them. Central Colorado was many miles north of upper New Mexico, some of the country they had to pass through was rough, rocky and timbered. The hope was that by the time they crossed into Colorado the remuda would be worked down enough to be tractable, which normally would be the case. Driven horses, like driven cattle, eventually settled down to a trail. The difference was that if something spooked horses they could swiftly scatter which cattle rarely could do.

By mid-afternoon while they were still in the burnt timber country, the horses came to water. Because their drovers hung back the horses tanked up, after which they were more readily controlled.

In fact as the warm day wore along the horses were allowed to graze as they walked along. As Heber said, better to be late getting home than to arrive with half the horses.

Neither of the drovers anticipated trouble, although with critters as easily panicked as loose-stock, anything could happen, and probably would sooner or later. Something as harmless as a covey of quail or prairie chickens suddenly exploding underfoot could cause a stampede.

Where they eventually came together riding on loose reins, Heber said the burnt timber country made him uncomfortable. It was forlorn and gloomy for a fact. They had not encountered it the ride south, they had passed by miles easterly.

Jeff had his own grim thoughts and only nodded agreement. He saw some of those large, lazily circling birds and said, "*Sopilotes.*" Heber looked up frowning. "Buzzards." Jeff shrugged. "Messicans call 'em *sopilotes.*"

Some Spanish had also rubbed off on Heber. A little farther along he said, "They call eggs *huevos*, an' horses *caballos*, an' that business about old Alvarez, they say 'Don' an make it sound like dawn. They're different, Jeff."

Heber got no reply to that. Jeff remembered what Tiburcio had said. He was unable to accept it after the massacre and that *ley fuga* business, but in other ways — well hell, they mounted a horse from the left side, they loped, rarely trotted a horse, they rode centre-fire rigs, of course that horn the size of a supper plate was sort of silly . . . There *were* differences, but for the most part understandable ones.

They reached a grassy clearing among the dead trees. Heber studied the sky. It had been a long day. They could drive another hour or so, but this clearing had good feed and the lord knew when they would find as good a bedding-down place up ahead.

They hung back so the loose-stock would understand and scatter, which they did. Tired horses were usually hungry horses.

As they hobbled their personal mounts and up-ended saddles near their bedrolls, Heber fished a soggy gingham cloth from a saddlebag. "I don't know what the meat is. One of them stone-faced women back yonder give it to me."

Whatever it was, stringy or not, it had been cooked with pepper flavouring. It went down well, and as Heber said, most likely would stay down.

Jeff estimated they were close to thirty miles from the Alvarez place, maybe a tad more, the first few miles they had covered in record time.

After eating they sat back with stars as clear as glass overhead in a flawless sky. Heber said he would take first nighthawking. Neither of them thought the remuda would drift much. They also thought that, being barefoot horses, by the time they got out of the rough burnt timber country their feet would be worn tender enough for them to feel disinclined to run or scatter.

In fact as Heber saddled up to take the first night-watch, Jeff rolled into his soogans without a troubling thought. They had made good distance, the horses were settling into what should be a routine drive, the weather was holding, they had found grass and water . . . Jeff shed his hat, shellbelt and boots, settled in for what he thought would be half a night's sleep and counted stars until he dozed off.

There were coyotes in the westerly

distance, there were ground-skimming owls too, whose uncanny ability to navigate among dead trees went unnoticed because they skimmed past in silence.

Heber lit a smoke inside his hat on the far west side of the clearing, thought he had caught a glimpse of a fire southward, but when he looked again there was no fire.

He sat beside his dozing horse, only half alert when the animal suddenly raised its head looking southward, both ears pointing. He told the horse coyotes followed any scent of warm flesh, to go back to sleep.

He made out both the big dipper and the little dipper as he'd done dozens of times while nighthawking. His mind wandered back to the Alvarez place. Things which were strange to him seemed to be the kind of variation of the same things men did up north, which were required of a different kind of country.

Heber was inclined to be more

tolerant than his partner. He hadn't seen that massacre. Seeing something like that and hearing about it were not the same.

His horse shifted position until it was facing southeastward. It was still engrossed with a scent. It had to be a scent because it was too dark to see.

Heber had chill inside his coat so he stood up and swung his arms. Except for a few milling horses the night was quiet. He watched a big bay gelding turn several times like a dog before folding his front legs and dropping down with a grunt. He had always thought lying down for horses was such an awkward thing to do, maybe that was why they slept standing up.

The bay horse had scarcely settled than his head came up, he bunched his muscles and sprang to his feet. He too was facing southeasterly.

Heber listened for coyotes. There was not a sound. Several other horses awakened and gazed southeasterly but for the most part these animals did not seem particularly interested, some of them lowered their heads and closed their eyes again.

Over east of the grassy place a horse nickered and was answered by a horse on Heber's side of the clearing. He stopped swinging his arms. The first horse to nicker had been over about where he and Jeff had made camp.

Loose-stock did not get that chummy with drovers. That horse had sounded as though he was about where Jeff was sleeping. Heber swung over his saddle and began a slow ride around the lower end of the remuda so as not to spook the horses, and picked his way watching ahead.

There was nothing to see, in particular there was no horse close to the lump that would be Jeff in his bedroll.

That cold feeling up his spine that had never entirely left Heber since they'd ridden through the burnt timber was still there. He reined to a stop, sat with both hands atop the saddle horn and waited, then softly called his partner's name. The reply came as a snore, a space of quiet, then another snore.

Heber kneed his mount ahead, dismounted just short of the camp and knelt to hobble the horse. It was time for Jeff to take over anyway.

Movement across the bedroll and out a short distance caught Heber's attention. He was bending over, hobbles in hand, head up, eyes wide as the movement came a few paces closer. Heber saw the gun aimed at him before he could make the man out clearly.

Recognition struck him dumb. It was the man who had robbed him, had split his scalp, and the Mexican was smiling as he waited for Heber to make a decision.

It was too dark to see if there were other Mexicans farther back, but there had been the other time. He slowly straightened up with a pair of hobbles dangling in his right hand. He could not have dropped them then and gone for his gun if he had wanted to. All the gently smiling Mexican had to do was raise his hammer and let it fall.

Heber sighed. Jeff snored again which the Mexican ignored but Heber could have kicked the bedroll. "Your move," he told the Mexican. He knew the man spoke English, he had used it the last time they met.

"Drop the gun, *amigo*."

As Heber moved to obey Jeff snored again. He let his sixgun fall. The Mexican relaxed and put his head a little to one side. "You have another gun," he said, making a statement of it, not a question.

"No other gun."

"A knife?"

Heber was tempted to say he was not a Mexican, he did not carry knives. Instead he shook his head. "Just my pocket knife."

The Mexican gestured with his pistol. Heber dug out the clasp knife and dropped it too.

"Your friend is a hard sleeper, no?"

"Right now I could choke him."

The Mexican's white teeth flashed. He said something in Spanish, several other Mexicans came forward out of the darkness . . . One of them leaned to lift away Jeff's folded shellbelt and Colt beside the bedroll.

The Mexican did not holster his gun but the barrel drooped a little as he regarded Heber. "You are all right, then?"

"I got a bandage under my hat if that's what you mean."

One of the other Mexicans said, "Skull like stone, *jefe*, on that one."

The smiling Mexican was not as tall as Heber, in fact he was slightly shorter than his companions, and as Heber remembered, his complexion was lighter, which in darkness was more noticeable among his companions. Heber thought he recalled something else, he had been called 'capitan' when they had met before.

A hunch was firming up in Heber as he faced the Mexicans across the blissfully snoring man in the bedroll between them. "We don't have any money," he told the fair-complexioned man.

The answer surprised him. "No, but you got it back from those bandits. But with the help of Don Alvarez y Pacheco. They stole it from me . . . We were tracking them when we saw you and your friend go after them with Don Alvarez's riders. So, we followed from a different direction, saw what happened in that low place, and followed you back . . . And now you have no money, Don Alvarez has it, but you have what we wanted in the first place. The remuda."

Jeff coughed, cleared his pipes and slowly sat up. He sat like stone for half a minute before the Mexican said, "*Buenas dias*. If you have a gun in those blankets I will shoot your head off."

Heber looked down. "He don't have a gun."

The Mexican gestured. "Throw back the blankets and stand up."

Jeff obeyed groggily. A Mexican grinned, he had Jeff's shellbelt and holstered Colt slung carelessly over his shoulder.

The lighter-complexioned man said something in Spanish and all but two of his companions faded back into darkness. Jeff and Heber could hear them mounting horses.

The smaller man with the sixgun motioned toward the ground with his Colt. "*Sentarse.*"

They sat on the ground. The Mexican smiled at them. "You learn quickly. *Bueno.*"

5

States of Confusion

THEY heard the remuda being roused in darkness. The vaqueros were riding a thin line across the northward area, the direction the horses were becoming accustomed to go. The vaqueros did everything without haste. It occurred to Heber that they were accomplished horsethieves. Only idiots and greenhorns stampeded horses, especially at night. These men barely raised their voices, rode at a walk, flailed a time or two with coiled riatas but did nothing to stampede the remuda.

Heber and Jeff heard the animals passing west of them back the way they had come. The Mexican with the gun in his hand also listened. Probably because he was more experienced at something like this than either of the men on ground, he could correctly interpret every sound. They must have pleased him because he hunkered regarding his prisoners and said,

"Your patrón should understand, when you get up there without the horses, that this is the fortune of war."

Jeff spoke disgustedly. "What war? There ain't no war, mister. This is plain out horse stealing."

The Mexican's smile dimmed as he became earnest. "There will be war, soon, friends. But to make a good war men must first be prepared."

Heber had been silently studying the fair-complexioned man. "I know it's not mannerly to ask personal questions, but don't many folks we've run across down here speak English as good as you do."

The Mexican's smile indicated that he felt complimented. "I was born . . . Do you know a town in Colorado called Durango? That's where I was born. My father had a store there. I went to school . . . They called me a 'greaser' and worse. I went to Mexico." The man shrugged.

Heber nodded. "You're a captain in the Mex Army?"

The Mexican laughed. "Not the army, no. I am a captain of Rurales." He made a little gesture. "I have to dress like everyone else up here. I can't wear my uniform, can I?"

They looked at him through a period of silence remembering what they had heard about Rurales. Eventually Heber asked if the others were also Rurales.

"Yes, but dressed like everyday vaqueros. Up here even Mexicans don't like us."

A rider walked up, dismounted and spoke quietly. The Rurale captain arose, holstered his sixgun and sent the other men to bring up his mount. As he waited he said, "This time, *amigos*, no one gets hurt." When his horse arrived he mounted with the other man and said something that kept Heber and

Jeff seated as they watched the two Mexicans grow faint in darkness.

"We take your guns and your horses. *Adios, gringos!*"

Jeff sighed listening to fading riders. "Adios, you son of a bitch. The next time we meet I'm goin' to slit your ear an' pull your arm through it . . . Get up, Heber, it's one hell of a long walk back."

As they trudged southward back among the burnt timber Heber said nothing. They had lost the money, now they had lost the horses as well. An hour into their southward walk Heber said, "It's closer if we angle a little southeasterly to that town. Alvarez's place is half again as far. Those horse thieves will be so far off we'll never find them if we head for the Alvarez yard."

Jeff was trying to remember if he had heard how far it was to the Mexican border. If anyone had mentioned it he could not recall. It probably was not going to make any difference anyway.

They angled southeasterly with only a vague idea where Adelentado was. By dawn they could see roofs, when the sun was climbing they smelled smoke. By the time they entered Adelentado from the north their feet hurt, their feet hurt from unaccustomed walking, and they were both cold and hungry. People stared as they passed. There was heat from a small iron stove in the *juzgado* but Fausto Molinero was not there.

They sat for a while, rested, then helped themselves to a pair of cups of coffee from the contents of a small pot atop the stove.

When the *jefe* walked in he seemed surprised. They explained what had happened, roughly where it had happened as best they could, and when they mentioned Rurales the local constable stared.

"How do you know they were Rurales?" he asked.

Jeff replied. "Because their captain told us. He said they were dressed like everyone else, otherwise they couldn't have passed through. He said they wanted our horses for some trouble that was coming in Mexico."

"What was his name?" Molinero asked.

"He never said his name," Heber replied. "He was a short man, light-skinned, maybe thirty, thirty-five. We met him once before."

They explained about that other meeting. They also told Molinero about the pursuit of bandits, the massacre and returning to the Alvarez place with money for the horses.

Molinero sat down. He looked tired and it was only mid-morning. "You could have gone back to Don Alvarez," he said, sounding, and looking, as though he wished they had. "If they took the horses early last night . . . The border is not too far from here."

Someone called loudly from the roadway. *Jefe* Molinero arose to look out the only window, which was deeply set and had four steel bars on the outside. He stood so long Jeff and Heber exchanged a look, arose and went to crowd close.

Two dusty, rumpled soldiers in faded blue were at the rack out front. They were lean, bronzed men in need of a shave and some soap. They stepped to the jailhouse door and pushed inside.

Jeff and Heber nodded. Molinero spoke in Spanish. One soldier would have answered in the same language but the other one, greying, hawk-faced and pale-eyed held up a hand. "You *habla* English?" he asked. Molinero nodded as the officer looked for a place to sit, crossed to a bench along the north wall, dropped down and shoved out long legs as he studied Heber and Jeff.

"Then let's talk English," he roughly said, returning his pale gaze to Fausto Molinero. "I'm Captain Mead. This here is Lieutenant Morrison. We got a company stabling at the lower end of town." Captain Mead paused to glance toward Heber and Jeff again.

"You fellers live in Adelentado?" he asked.

Jeff shook his head, explained how they happened to be in town, and when he had finished the two officers stared at him without a word. Heber sat down again. He explained about their first encounter with the Mexican horse thieves. He also recounted what had happened later, and how they had finally gotten their remuda lined out for the drive to the Dixon ranch up north.

The captain eyed *Jefe* Molinero. "They told you all this?"

"Yes."

"And you been sittin' on your butt, *alguacil*?"

"But they only got here, *Capitan*."

"And you're still sittin' on your butt," the captain exclaimed, and leaned forward. "Let me tell you something. You gawddamned beaners sit an' moan, cry for the army an' bastards like those Rurales could be in your back room an' you'd be sittin' like you are now."

Jeff and Heber were still. *Jefe* Molinero seemed about to speak. The captain stood up and levelled a finger at him. "We're the scoutin' party, *alguacil*. There's a troop down along the border. There've been other complaints. We know what they're fixin' to do down there . . . damned fool beaners." He swung toward Jeff and Heber. "Gents, if those bastards get close to the border the army's goin' to come down on them like the sky opened up. Horses make dust, Messicans drivin' horses toward the border from up here . . . " The captain showed his teeth. "You want your horses back? Hire some mounts and go back with us. If we don't get 'em back we'll go down over the damned border and get as many as you lost."

Captain Mead went to the door, ignored Molinero and waited. Jeff arose first, then Heber also stood up. The captain addressed his junior officer. "Charley, go with 'em. See they get mounted."

As they left the jailhouse the constable was still sitting, looking more tired now than ever.

The lieutenant went with Heber and Jeff to the only place that looked like a livery barn. It had corrals out back and on both sides. The proprietor was a large, heavy Mexican with a thin slit of a mouth and black eyes. The lieutenant told him in Spanish what they wanted, and he smiled straight into the larger man's eyes. *"Now! Pronto!"*

Jeff and Heber did as they'd done at the jailhouse, they did not move, they almost didn't breathe. The liveryman was four inches taller and thirty pounds heavier than the lieutenant, and his expression was fierce. He and the officer stared at each other until the lieutenant smiled and reached for the big revolver on his right side.

The liveryman turned and moved swiftly. He took them out back and showed them several horses. The two he offered were large, muscular animals with little sullen eyes and it seemed

81

that both ears came out of the same hole.

Heber and Jeff made their own selection, which the large, swarthy man did not like but he led the horses inside to be saddled.

The captain appeared with troopers behind him. He called from the roadway, he was leading the junior officer's horse.

Jeff and Heber led their animals out front, turned them and swung over leather. The big Mexican glared but said nothing.

Captain Mead was not an individual to argue with, which was obvious. What was less clear but which became clear an hour down the trail, he was also familiar with the country, and with a job to do wasted no time in doing it.

The company rode southwesterly. They made good time. Mead detached a corporal to make contact ahead. He slackened gait and rode with Jeff and Heber asking questions.

They described the Rurale officer

but could only guess at the number of riders with him. "Six, eight, maybe ten, it was dark every time we met."

Captain Mead lighted a crooked, thin cigar, smoked for a short distance then removed the stogie and smiled. "They're stealin' weapons an' livestock all along this part of the border. We got reinforcements comin' from up north. This time, by gawd, if they raid up here durin' their damned war, we'll cut 'em off on the ride back. This time, by gawd, we had advance warning."

The lieutenant said something in Spanish. Captain Mead stood in his stirrups, cigar tightly clamped. He did not ease down; nothing he ever seemed to do was done gently, he dropped down hard and growled in Spanish to the lieutenant. Heber nudged Jeff. "For a feller who don't like Messicans or their language . . ."

Jeff smiled and nodded as they watched the lieutenant lope in the direction the earlier scout had taken. Captain Mead raised his arm and brought it sharply down. The entire company broke over into a lope. Jeff looked back. No real attempt was made to dress the lines. He also noticed something else. There was not a single sword among the cavalrymen, and a few other things, cocked hats, loosened collars, soiled gauntlets . . . Hell, this bunch of U.S. horse-soldiers looked and acted more like guerillas. One thing was obvious, Captain Mead was a saddle-and-carbine soldier. If he had been anything less the ranks would have been aligned, hats would have been straight, uniforms would not be loose at the gullet.

Jeff thought Mead's troopers and their captain were more nearly irregular comrades than regular soldiers.

Heber leaned. "What did he call the constable back there?"

Jeff shrugged. "I tried to pronounce it like he did. I'll never learn that damned language . . . "

Captain Mead was riding standing

in his stirrups. He never once glanced back. His hat was pulled low, his bronzed, hawk-like face was stone-set and that ridiculous cigar jutted upwards.

The day was hot but except for sweat-shiny horses it seemed to have little effect. A red-faced burly man with faded sergeant's stripes and a peeling nose called out and pointed.

There was dust, a big cloud of it due west. The border was southward but if the soldiers knew where it was, and they most certainly did, they seemed more interested in continuing westward than southward. Heber told Jeff if that dust was their remuda, something sure as hell must have delayed the horse thieves. By this time of day they should have been much farther along on their way to Old Mexico.

The lieutenant returned but that scout sent out earlier did not. It seemed to Jeff he and Heber worried more about this than the officers did. There was a good reason for this but for the time being only the officers knew what it was.

They closed fast on that moving banner of dun dust. When the troop slackened down to a steady walk the dust was less than a mile ahead which on a clear day made any kind of movement visible, if not in detail at least in substance. Neither Jeff nor Heber spoke, but the cause of that dust was a big band of loose stock moving too fast to be cattle but not distinguishable yet as driven horses.

The lieutenant spurred ahead again. Every eye was on him right up until he halted. It was impossible to see why he had stopped, but moments later, after another hundred or so yards had been covered by the troopers and the captain held up his hand for a halt, they saw the dirty white puffs moments before they heard the gunshots.

The lieutenant sat his horse until the main party arrived, then gestured as he spoke to the captain. Most of his gesturing was in a southerly direction.

While this palaver was in progress another banner of dust appeared farther back, and perhaps because this puzzled the officers, the troop did not move.

Jeff tipped his hat forward squinting hard in the direction of the northerly dust. He was the first to make a tentative identification. It was based on the direction from which the farther-away riders were coming. He told Heber he thought he had the answer as to why those Rurales had not got down over the border hours earlier; they had driven the Dixon horses southward and on the way had picked up more horses, a lot more horses.

Heber made a guess. "From Alvarez's range?"

Jeff did not answer. He finally could make out the second band of riders. The things which would have made it possible to positively identify them were lacking because of distance, but the way they rode said 'vaqueros' to him.

He rode up to the officers told them what he thought was happening, and while they listened they continued to remain in place.

As Jeff rode back Heber also made a guess. "They got reinforcements comin' up from the border."

Heber was right but it would be a while before proof arrived, meanwhile the officers sat watching right up until that first big cloud of dust seemed to widen, to turn back into itself, then, finally, the captain signalled for the advance to be resumed, and led off in a walk.

What neither Jeff nor Heber had seen was the reason that headlong stampede toward Mexico had spread, turned back upon itself, seemed to scatter in confusion. Not until they saw the blue line and the tiny puffs of soiled smoke.

This time there had been no dust. The troopers from closer to the border had not made a headlong rush as the others had. They had clearly fanned out in skirmish order and begun an advance straight across the line the horse thieves were taking to the border.

The big remuda and its drovers were caught from three sides. Captain Mead's detachment did not enter the action. It achieved its purpose by simply appearing from the east to box in the horse thieves from that direction. They were already boxed in from the direction of the border and from the direction they had come, northerly.

As the skirmish increased with closer contact between pursued and pursuers, Captain Mead continued his steady slow advance toward increasing clouds of dust, until he was close enough to distinctly hear gunfire. He did not hasten nor slacken. Jeff swore under his breath. The occasional shadowy figures, more wraith than real, which showed for a moment then were lost again in the dust, could not be positively identified.

They were such indistinct and brief targets it was unwise to shoot. Even blue uniforms were rarely distinguishable.

Captain Mead raised his arm some

distance away, rested both hands on the hornless swells of his McClellen saddle and sat like a statue.

Heber and Jeff sweated and fidgetted. They could of course have left the soldier column to join the fight. But as agitated as they both were, simple reason warned against riding into a mêlée where chances were excellent that if soldiers did not mistake them for horse thieves, the horse thieves might think they were at the very least possemen, while the vaqueros would possibly shoot them for no other reason than because they were in front of them in the dust.

Captain Mead spoke aside to his junior officer. "Did you ever see a finer example of the difference between discipline and rowdyism? They'll shoot each other before this is over."

It was army analysis, which did not make it correct.

6

Raton Pass

THE dust made the difference. The thieves fled west, the only direction from which they had not been fired at. Otherwise, the fight dwindled only very slowly. Another difficulty was the horses, there were several hundred, panicked, running blindly. As the firing dwindled the horses became more dangerous.

They, too, had been confused by dust. Being cowards by nature they fled first one way, then another way.

By the time Captain Mead decided to move ahead riders were trying to get south of the area to prevent horses from fleeing blindly down over the border. As Jeff and Heber watched this, it became increasingly obvious those horsemen were vaqueros, but while this was reassuring to them, it was neither reassuring nor agreeable to the soldiers who had been firing at anyone riding a Mexican saddle or who looked like a Mexican.

Not until Jeff and Heber went flinging into the confusion yelling at the top of their lungs did the soldiers seem to hesitate. During this time Captain Mead stormed up and roared at Jeff and Heber. They roared back that the Mexican horsemen trying to turn the horses north were not the thieves. Captain Mead accepted this for the obvious reason that the horsemen were for a fact, preventing the remuda from continuing southward. He and his lieutenant rode among the other soldiers yelling for them to stop firing.

For half an hour confusion, noise and dust prevailed. Only when the loose stock was heading back the way it had come did the soldiers finally stop pressing the fight.

They stopped panting to watch

several vaqueros keeping up pressure on the remuda going north. Jeff and Heber were standing beside their animals also watching, when a rider appeared behind them and called a greeting.

It was Tiburcio. He was sweaty, covered with dust and so weary that when he dismounted he stumbled, but he managed a smile as he said, "Don Alvarez and the others went after those riders of other people's horses . . . Where did you find the soldiers?"

They told him how they had happened to be out here. A tall vaquero walked up and handed Tiburcio a bottle of tequila, which the older man drank from and almost immediately seemed restored. He leaned across the seat of his saddle watching the soldiers come together. There seemed to be an argument among the officers. Heber made a grimace. He had no idea who the other officer was but he would have bet a good horse he knew who would win the argument.

Tiburcio was still watching the knot of soldiers when he said, "They were greedy. If they had kept going with only a few more miles to the border, they would have made it with your horses, but no, they had to make a sweep through our range and pick up our remuda as well." Tiburcio turned. "In broad daylight. If Don Alvarez catches them . . ."

Jeff and Heber nodded about that. They knew what would have happened.

Captain Mead and his shadow, the lieutenant, walked over. He nodded at Tiburcio and addressed Heber and Jeff. "You can find the horses and take your cut, I suppose." He paused to spit dust before saying the rest of it. "We're going back. One detail will continue after the Rurales."

Tiburcio spoke. "My patrón is chasing them. He will overtake them."

Captain Mead turned, gazed at the old vaquero from an expressionless face. "Who are you?"

"Tiburcio Reyes, señor, I am the

94

man of Don Alvarez y Pacheco, whose horses most of those animals belong to . . . Who are you?"

Tiburcio's usual congeniality was lacking. He had encountered this situation many times before during his long life.

He and the hawk-faced officer regarded each other for seconds before the officer said who he was. Jeff and Heber could almost feel the antagonism. Tiburcio acknowledged the introduction without a nod as he said, "I am an old man, señor. This is only the third time in all those years I have seen the army arrive when it was needed."

None of the gringos facing Tiburcio were sure whether he meant it as a compliment or not. His dark eyes were rock-hard and steady. Captain Mead stood a moment longer, then ignored Tiburcio to address Heber and Jeff. "Thanks for riding along." He walked away.

Tiburcio's cold stare followed him.

Under his breath he said something in Spanish.

The dust had settled, the sun bore down, thirst bothered men and animals. Tiburcio mounted his horse, considered the gringos a moment then smiled: "Now we have to cut out your remuda."

They rode north with him. Nothing was said about the Rurales or Don Alvarez in pursuit. By the time they reached the yard the sun was departing but the heat remained.

After caring for their animals they sought shade, later they went to the creek to bathe, by the time they returned the sun was gone leaving a kind of sultry daylight behind.

Tiburcio brought them to his *jacal* for supper. Several vaqueros drifted in, they spent the evening discussing the events of the day. Two had wounds, one in the fleshy part of the leg the other through his left ear, part of which had been cut away. His bandaged head reminded Heber of his own earlier wound, well along on the way to healing by now.

The general discussion agreed that for once the soldiers had been where they were most needed, but both Jeff and Heber noticed this was agreed to grudgingly. Clearly, the natives were not fond of the soldiers. It had not been too long before that the United States had won this part of the southwest, and much more, in a war with Mexico, and while many native New Mexicans, like *Californios*, had never felt favourable to the central Mexican government, neither did they feel comfortable with those who now owned their native land.

Heber and Jeff bedded down in the barn as they had done before. They said little, both were tired all the way through. Before the fight and the recovery of the horses, they had walked one hell of a distance to reach Adelentado.

The following two days they rode with the vaqueros cutting out their horses from the Alvarez loose stock. It was a dusty, tiring job. Nor were they always certain who owned particular animals, but what mattered to Tiburcio and his companions was that the same number would be corralled for the gringos.

During this time nothing was heard from Don Alvarez. His riders were guarded when they mentioned this in front of Jeff and Heber.

On the fourth day when they were ready to start north again Don Alvarez returned looking very much the worse for his intransigent pursuit.

He arrived at the corrals about the time the horses were to be headed north one more time. He had taken time to clean up and eat, but not to rest. When he met Jeff and Heber he smilingly said, "This time you should have no trouble. At least for as long as you are in New Mexico." Beyond that he shrugged.

Tiburcio came over, he and his patrón exchanged greetings before the old vaquero asked what neither Jeff or Heber had asked even though they wanted to the worst way.

Tiburcio spoke English. "You caught them, patrón?"

Don Alvarez replied shortly. "All but two. I think they got down over the border. I don't know. They just seemed to disappear. But we had the others. Eleven of them."

Tiburcio, Heber and Jeff looked steadily at Don Alvarez, eyes asking the obvious question. His gaze did not waver as he said, "We shot them."

Tiburcio was pleased. Jeff and Heber stared at Don Alvarez, who returned their stares. "We stood them in front of some large rocks, with their arms tied in back," Don Alvarez shrugged again. "I know what you do with horse thieves, you hang them, mostly wherever you catch them . . . Here, our trouble is that we have few trees." Don Alvarez smiled.

Tiburcio was called away by the vaqueros near the gate. They were ready to turn the horses loose. Heber and Jeff got astride. Everything was as before, when the gate was opened riders on both sides made certain the horses would run northward from the yard out across open country. Jeff and Heber rode in the rear, distant from each other in case there were early cut-backs.

In the yard vaqueros and Don Alvarez watched until dust and distance obscured the running horses and their drovers, then Don Alvarez turned, slapped two vaqueros lightly on the shoulder and struck out for the main-house. Once again, and with variations, he had started the gringos on their way. There surely could not be such an adverse fate to see either the gringos or the horses again.

For Jeff and Heber it was a repetitive performance. As before, when the remuda found water it was allowed to fill up before the drive continued north-ward. By afternoon they encountered the first forlorn skeletons of dead trees.

By the time they were ready to stop for the day they were very close to the same place they had stopped before, and had been intercepted by Rurales.

This time they did not make a fire. Also, this time, while one rode nighthawk the other remained awake watching and listening.

Neither of them thought these precautions were really necessary, but experience was a hard taskmaster. Even if one had slept, he would not have slept well.

In the morning they were on the trail with sunrise. There was a town westerly which they had bypassed on their way south. It was the place they had laughed about — a town named for a rat, *Raton*.

North of Raton for miles east and west, a very respectable range of mountains divided the lowland country from the highlands of Colorado.

Because they preferred not to travel up Raton Pass except in daylight, they made an early camp at a place where a spindly series of sump springs indicated there was an underground source of water.

There were burnt trees up here, but farther toward the mountains, that long-ago fire had not reached.

Jeff was beginning to be superstitious about the burnt timber country. He would have called it uneasiness, but the two feelings could be the same. He told Heber he'd breathe a hell of a lot easier when they could no longer see burnt trees.

As far as Heber was concerned, it was not just the ghostly dead trees, he would be more satisfied when they and the horses were completely out of New Mexico.

This night they had a small fire. They were only about ten miles, maybe a tad less, from the abrupt foothills that preceded those high upthrusts. At that distance they could reach the pass by mid-day, be up it and upon the high plateau by the time it would be necessary to make another night camp.

In the morning they had to waste a little time because some of the horses had drifted. By the time they were ready to aim for Raton Pass the sun was high, there was increasing heat, and the horses while fresh enough to be troublesome, moved along scuffing dust as though they were also willing to leave New Mexico.

When they started up the pass with its high narrow walls, there was only one direction and that was dead ahead. Heber and Jeff rode in the drag. They rolled smokes, studied the high upthrusts on both sides and speculated about who had found the pass, and had widened it and maintained it since.

The road was crooked, generally following around places where dynamiting to make the road straight would have resulted in blocking it. But the trail was wide, in fact in places a wagon could have navigated it. If there was a drawback it was that there were no places wide enough for two wagons to pass, let alone bands of driven livestock.

The drovers would normally have a point rider up ahead, but only if there were more than two drovers. Wagoneers had resolved this matter long ago by mounting bells on an attachment that rose about the names of lead teams. In places such as Raton Pass with its high sides, ringing bells could be heard over great distances.

Loose horses with no point rider to follow, moseyed along indifferent to possible meetings up ahead.

The sun had passed over the road in its deep cleft, shadows were in the canyon, the sky overhead remained an illuminated shade of blue, which was how drovers over the years had estimated the time of day — plus or minus an hour or so, because of the steady incline the horses trudged steadily, there was no compulsion among them to go any faster. They were sweating. The grade was steep, but between its bottom and top the grade was never abrupt, just steadily rising.

As far as Heber and Jeff were concerned, if this road continued all the way to their destination they would have been pleased, but of course it did not continue beyond an ultimate debouchment on the high plains, upper country.

The horses were strung out a considerable distance. The drovers only occasionally during a straight stretch, were able to see the leaders. For that reason when the leaders stopped considerable time was required for the bottleneck to be felt all the way back where Heber and Jeff were riding.

The overhead sky was still alight but now the brilliance was fading as the sun moved farther westerly on its downward course.

There was an indication that the horses were beginning to close up on one another. Stoppage far ahead was finally filtering back.

Jeff looked at the canyon sides; if

there had been a game trail which would enable a rider to get around the remuda to its head, he would have used it.

But the walls were nearly vertical.

Heber blocked a retrograde movement of the horses. As pressure built he yelled to Jeff he would try passing up through the remuda to the head of it, to find out what had caused the halt.

This could be accomplished providing Heber rode very slowly and did not crowd the loose animals. He struck out with Jeff watching his progress.

The horses pressed as far as they could to allow the rider to pass them on the trail. There was no serious attempt to whirl away, which would possibly have started a stampede back down out of the canyon. Both drovers were thankful for that even as they both understood that the reason was simply that the loose stock had been steadily climbing for miles. Their legs were up to it but their lungs had been taxed most of the way; they were in no shape, and in no mood, to break away and run.

For Jeff Forman the wait was long and tedious. The horses accepted the halt with equine resignation. Fortunately, as the sun had departed while it was still hot in the canyon, there was no direct heat.

The longer Jeff blocked the downgrade the more restless he became. It would be essential that they get out of the canyon and, hopefully, to water, before nightfall.

The horses were less upset because of the delay. They probably welcomed it.

Without being aware of it, Jeff was being watched by a horseman overhead on the west side of the canyon. He sat up there like a statue with a Winchester balanced across his lap.

Jeff was concerned with what was ahead, not just the dozing horses but his partner. Because he had no clear idea how far ahead Heber might have had to ride, he worried less about his partner than he did about the prolonged delay.

The end came abruptly. Horses began coming back down the canyon, not in haste but purposefully, the way animals moved who were being driven.

Jeff could see them returning before the horses nearest him felt the pressure, but inevitably they did, which caused them to crowd closer to the man blocking their southerly way.

Jeff was worried, he yelled and stood his ground. The horses began bunching, facing him, a few bold ones making little feints in the direction of the mounted man blocking their way.

He was fully occupied, did not look up, which probably would not have mattered by this time anyway, but that motionless rider high above dismounted without haste, knelt to take a good rest, snugged back his carbine at the same moment one of the distressed animals, an ugly-headed big rawboned bay horse, pawed and charged. Jeff swung to block him at the precise moment the overhead gunman fired.

Jeff saw the Roman-nosed big bay horse go down as though he'd been pole-axed.

He had only a moment to watch that happen, and another moment to look quickly up where a little puff of gunsmoke appeared. The next moment the gunshot, magnified by the canyon's walls until it sounded as loud as a cannon, started the stampede.

Jeff reacted instantly. He whirled his mount and led the charge back down the canyon. Most of the way he rode twisted sideways looking back.

Now, there was thick dust, he could see no farther than about fifty yards. That full distance and farther panicked horses were stampeding.

He kept ahead, praying hard that his horse would not stumble. If that happened he and his mount would be pounded to mincemeat by the blind-running animals farther back.

7

One More Damned Time!

IF it hadn't been stifling in the canyon the wild race would have reached the lower, more open country with horses and Jeff Forman, sweating rivers and pumping their lungs like bellows. The distance could have been measured in miles.

Where it was possible to do so, the remuda spread out, still running in panic but no longer able to maintain the same speed.

Jeff angled eastward. His idea was to prevent the horses from going in that direction, to keep them running in the direction they were familiar with.

It worked fairly well, he lost a few head but the main race was back in the direction of the burnt hills. By this time the horses may have had another motive; they knew where water was down there.

Jeff finally stopped, stepped to the ground, loosened the cinch so his panting mount could breathe better, and wiped sweat off his face as he watched dust ride behind the stampede.

He waited half an hour for Heber to come down the trail. When he did not appear Jeff turned back up the canyon. The loose stock would find water and rest by it. At least until the following morning.

He wanted to push his animal but refrained, the horse had been used hard enough.

Dusk was close by the time he reached the place where horse tracks ended. There were several large rocks on the east side. He dismounted, led the horse up the trail to be certain the remuda had not gone north of this place, then turned back with shadows forming in the canyon, and the heat slackening slightly. His fear was solid.

Someone had tried to roll several of the embedded big rocks into the road, and had been unsuccessful. While he was groping among the rocks a thirsty horse nickered. It was tied by the reins to a measly little sickly tree on the east side of the road among the boulders.

Jeff stopped at sight of Heber's animal. The carbine was in the boot. He had to force himself to resume the search. He encouraged himself by remembering that he had not heard a gunshot, but of course with bends in the trail and the distance, he probably would not have heard it anyway.

A rattle of small stones caught his attention. He leaned on a shoulder-high boulder and looked behind it. Heber stared back. He had been bound and gagged, his sixgun was missing, his belt had been used to bind both ankles, his bandanna handkerchief had been used to tie both wrists behind his back. He had been gagged with a soiled piece of grey cloth.

Jeff was so relieved not to have found

Heber dead that he smiled as he knelt to set his partner free. Heber sat up rubbing his wrists as he stared at Jeff. "That son of a bitch is indestructible!"

"Who?"

"That damned Rurale captain. He caught me like a little kid ridin' up here without any idea . . . I thought I heard a distant gunshot down yonder; are you all right?"

"Yeah. I didn't see him. He was atop the canyon to the west. He missed me an' killed a big bay horse . . . Then the race began, with me out front and promisin' gawd a whole lot of things if he'd keep my horse from stumbling. The remuda headed back down to the burnt timber country an' I came lookin' for you."

Heber continued to stir circulation in his wrists as he said, "There were four of them. One rode off after they threw down on me. The captain laughed. I guess I stared like he was a ghost. He said him and three others out-run Don Alvarez and turned back north . . . I'll tell you one thing about that damned screwt, he sure don't give up easy."

Jeff helped his partner to stand. While Heber was getting circulation back in his lower legs, Jeff went after his horse. While he was doing this it occurred to him that the captain and what was left of his Rurale company, had been after the horses again, had known which way Heber and Jeff had been driving them before, and had beaten them to Raton Pass where they set up their ambush.

What all this meant, sure as gawd had made sour apples, was that the captain would pick up the remuda and start for the border with it again.

As Heber had said, that was one Mexican who did not have sense enough to give up. Maybe he had a particular reason; maybe he had been promised a promotion if he brought horses back. Maybe he did it for money, or just to salvage his self respect after what had happened to him down near the border.

Maybe a whole passel of things. Jeff led the horse back, waited until his partner was astride, then started down the darkening canyon.

"He lost a lot of his crew when Don Alvarez caught them."

"Yes he did, just about wiped out his company."

"Heber, why didn't he shoot you?"

"I figure it was maybe because the noise would have stampeded the remuda before he was ready . . . I'll tell you one thing, Jeff, the next time I see that son of a bitch, I won't care which way he's facing."

Jeff rode in silence almost to the mouth of the canyon before speaking again. "You been down here too long, Heber. You're beginnin' to sound like a Messican."

They rode until midnight on dead-tired, thirsty horses. They heard loose stock near a warm-water creek and stopped there for a while. As they were tending the horses Heber blew out a ragged curse. He did not want to have

115

to ride back south again. He said it was like one of those revolving doors folks had back east. Start north, get runover, go back south, start north again, get caught flat-footed in a damned canyon, and ride south again.

Jeff left his partner with the horses, took his carbine and walked southward. He encountered horses along the creek. Even in poor light he could make out the Alvarez brand.

There was no sign of the dogged Mexicans but he continued scouting.

Eventually he turned back. The Rurales were out there somewhere. They wouldn't abandon the horses they had taken such risks to get, had been badly hurt, damned near wiped out by the soldiers on the brink of racing over the border, which was sanctuary to just about anyone who could cross in one piece, and now had the horses heading toward the border again.

Heber was sleeping when Jeff reached the camp. There was not even a break in his breathing despite the noise Jeff made.

There was one thing they could rely upon, that Mexican officer would have the remuda heading south again at first light. As Jeff shed his boots and hat but did not unroll his blankets, he wondered about something else — would that Rurale drive across the Alvarez range trying to add to his stolen remuda again? Probably not. He had not impressed Jeff as that much of a fool.

But sure as hell he would drive straight for the border with the Dixon horses.

Heber interrupted Jeff's ponderings without raising up. "There's only one way we'll even see those horses again, partner. That's if we saddle up right now and keep riding south until daylight. With luck we'll be south of them when that damned Mex horsethief comes south. My guess is that this'll be our last chance."

Jeff pulled on his boots groaned to

himself and stood up. They had to have fresh animals.

He led off with his rope because he knew where the horses were and Heber did not. But finding loose stock was one thing, catching two of them was another thing. This had to be accomplished with as little noise as possible.

They had no idea where the Rurales were, but for a fact they would not be bedded down too far from the remuda.

Jeff found a grey mare, got almost up to her before she sidled away. He tried twice more before he found a rawboned tall horse with the kind of skimpy mane and forelock which was usual among thoroughbreds or near-thoroughbreds. This time the horse allowed himself to be 'jockeyed' and eventually caught. Unlike most cold-blooded horses, it was the heritage of well-bred horses to be ambivalent enough about two-legged creatures to allow themselves to be caught.

Heber was longer stalking the animals. The one he eventually caught did not fight once the rope was on him, but as he walked behind Heber he looked steadily at the man. He showed no fear. Under normal circumstances they would have turned him loose but time was important so they went back, saddled both animals, walked them a short distance before mounting — a sound practice with any strange horse — then mounted.

The big thoroughbred walked along head up, interested in what he was supposed to do. Heber's animal walked behind the thoroughbred, which seemed a tractable thing to do and it was, as long as there was a horse ahead to be followed.

They rode through the burnt forest bearing westerly so as to get far enough in that direction to avoid upsetting the loose stock or awakening the Rurales.

It was a long ride. A mile or so on their way cold set in. The horses still marched along, one behind the other.

119

Jeff began veering easterly which he thought would put them back in the area the remuda would use coming south.

They rode for several hours, without haste but without stopping either. When a sickly glow spread along the easterly horizon, they sought a high place where, after sunrise they would be able to see the oncoming remuda.

For the first time since mounting they rode atop a low landswell where those silent, blackened dead trees were particularly thick, halted, dismounted and, trailing a rein, walked back to the edge of the high place where they commanded an excellent view of the northward country.

Where there should have been dust there was fresh, newday brilliance with perfect visibility for miles. Heber swore. Jeff went forward for a wider view. It was the same, there was no dust, no Rurales and no loose stock.

He went back, leaned across his saddle and groaned inwardly. Heber said, "The sons of bitches took another route." He swore with feeling before also saying, "We under-estimated that Rurale."

Jeff's remark had nothing much to do with the Mexicans. "They're goin' south. That's where they come from an' that's the way they're goin' to return."

Heber scowled. "Did you just figure that out, for Chris'sake? Of course they's heading south. That's where the border is, isn't it?"

"Due south there's somethin' else," Jeff stated. "Soldiers patrolling. Maybe Alvarez's down there too. Maybe even that tinhorn lawman from Adelentado."

Heber's brow cleared. "Some other route?"

Jeff nodded and turned to mount the tall horse. "Yeah, that's got to be it. Some other route but in a different way — still southward. And unless I'm wrong as hell, we're still south of them."

He led off down the hill, turned back

121

the way they had come, got up where the remuda had been, and without conversation sashayed until they found the route the remuda had taken, and it was westerly. They followed it long enough to be certain, then paralleled the wide jumble of barefoot horse tracks until Heber gestured. "They got to turn south somewhere. All they're doin' now is goin' parallel with the border."

Jeff eased the horse into an easy lope, westerly but also southward. According to his estimate the longer the thieves drove the loose stock west, the better would be the chances of their pursuers to get below them by riding anglingly in the direction of the border. With luck they should be down there before the Rurales felt safe enough to alter course and head due south.

It was chancy, Jeff said, and they might not make contact, but almost anything was better than riding all the way back to the home place and have to tell Mister Dixon they had not only lost his money, but also his horses.

The sun rose and for a few hours there was no heat. The man on the leggy big thoroughbred horse and his partner directly behind on the other animal, made dust only when they loped, which they did as often as it seemed necessary in order to get down near the border as soon as possible.

They came across someone's abandoned dug-well where a square adobe structure, built to withstand sieges faced eastward. It had two front window openings, otherwise there was only a thick door. It was hanging open. The man who had built this fort of a home, had observed every rule of survival in a country where Indians, border-jumpers, Rurales, outlaws, crisscrossed — except one. He had sodded his roof, which was fine except that sod roofs grew grass and dry grass burned hot. All that remained of the roof lay inside the four stout walls. It told its own story.

The dug-well had water. Jeff dropped

a stone and heard it splash. They had to make a bucket out of some wood rounds which had been hollowed out, probably to serve as buckets. They had been lying dry so long there were veiny cracks that leaked water not quite as fast as Heber and Jeff could haul it up using lariats, but thirsty horses were indifferent to the difficulties the men had to surmount to tank them up. Each horse drank several buckets empty. Heber was sweating hard when they hauled up the last bucket for themselves. When Jeff noted that the wood was swelling, less water was leaking out, Heber drank, used a soaked bandanna on the back of his neck and his face as he said, "Fine. Now that we don't need to haul 'em up any more."

They left the haunted place bearing slightly more south than west. The heat was increasing so they had to favour the animals more, something which exasperated the hell out of them.

They had been riding steadily since

shortly after midnight. Until the sun was high enough to show such things, they watched for dust but saw none. Not until they passed an isolated but inhabited small wooden house with cottonwood trees shading it. This place was not as defensible as the other place had been, but it evidently had a good well. Cottonwoods only grew in shallow-water country.

They passed well southward but two men with rifles came outside to stand watching. Heber was squinting northward. Jeff was gazing in the direction of the homestead. Because he was looking northward he saw the distant but unmistakable lazy stand of thin dust.

When Heber saw it he crowed. "Behind us and a hell of a distance north. We done it, partner, we got below the sons of bitches before they figured it was safe to turn south."

Jeff eased down to a steady walk. The highly intelligent animal he was riding also walked along looking up where the dust was. Heber's animal was concerned with only thing, the rear-end of the horse ahead of him. Neither of the horsemen noticed that.

Jeff began another change of course. There were no boundary markers. Those there were, mounds of rocks painted white at long intervals, were most often found near towns.

Southward the land was the same. There could have been towns down there, but if there were they were not in sight. It would have been easier to place the border if there had been towns. Mex towns did not look like gringo towns.

Jeff and his partner only knew the border was a fair distance south. How far, exactly, did not worry them. The horse thieves would know, at least in general, and give or take a mile or so was acceptable.

Jeff and Heber intended to explode in front of the loose stock in order to stampede it back the way it had come. Whichever side of the border they were on when they accomplished this — *if* they accomplished it — would be immaterial as long as the remuda ran north and kept running in that direction.

They were concentrating on the dust, gauging distances, considering chances of success, and did not notice two mounted men far behind clearly following. Across their laps each rider had a rifle, not a carbine.

Jeff slackened pace, Heber's horse, the inherent follower, immediately did the same thing without any pressure on his reins.

Heber made a guess. "Mile behind us." He sounded almost triumphant.

Jeff was beginning to scan the countryside ahead about where a meeting would occur providing the Rurales finally swung south, which they eventually did for the best of all reasons, they were many miles west of where the soldier-patrols had been, and even farther from the Alvarez ranch.

There were few trees, mostly in the

wrong place, either down in Mexico or far enough north to be close to the shuffling-along remuda.

Tired horses dragged their hind feet. Thirsty, tired horses walked almost mechanically ahead of drovers, dragging their hind hooves and walking with their heads down.

Jeff made a guess the remuda would come fairly close to some sandstone rocks lying in a jumble about a half mile ahead. He told Heber he figured the loose stock would pass either on the east or west side of the field of rocks.

They loped in among those rocks, dismounted, put their animals where they would be safest — and for the first time saw that pair of distant men with long-guns across their laps.

Heber was annoyed. "Those damned fools is goin' to be in the line of fire if the Messicans drive past on the west side."

Jeff squinted before shaking his head. "They stopped. Not even a cannon could reach them from here."

"Who are they?" Heber asked irritably. "You reckon they been following us?"

"Maybe those two fellers with rifles we saw back yonder at that homestead."

Heber glared his hostility. "Like buzzards; trailin' us to be in on the kill. We couldn't match them, Jeff. You got no hand-gun and our carbines won't reach that far."

Heber brightened. "Maybe when the Messicans get down here that'll scare them off."

8

Dust, Blood and Horses

THE horsethieves arrived but it was a long wait. The remuda had been denied adequate rest during their see-saw course of travel the last few days. They were not only tired but their hooves were worn down. They had become increasingly tender-footed as time passed.

Heber recognised several of the tucked-up animals. He wagged his head over their condition. The shape they were in now, hell, they couldn't be pushed hard which meant he and Jeff would be on this trail for weeks longer than they or Mister Dixon expected.

Jeff's interest was high. Primarily, he was concerned about the remuda and the men driving it, one on each wing, one riding ahead at point, and one eating dust far back.

Heber growled until Jeff turned. Those two horsemen in the distance with rifles in their laps, had not moved. Evidently they had seen, and were watching the loose stock. They were more than ever like statues with the sun at their back.

They were no immediate threat, they were too far even for rifles, but they were annoying just for the way they sat out there watching the show-down unfold.

Heber was spitting cotton. He had settled into a nice nest of thick rocks. The trouble with sandstone was that it exploded like shrapnel under gunfire.

Jeff used a filthy sleeve to push sweat off his face. He estimated the distance from the rocks to the lead rider to be maybe a half a mile. Maybe a tad less because he could see the man fairly well in detail, and did not recognise anything about him except his vaquero attire and his *esilla vaquero* with its distinctive white rawhide cover over the tree and the huge saddlehorn.

He settled into place, rested his carbine, shook off annoying perspiration and while conscious of those distant observers was really only concerned with that Mex point-rider. He knew what his partner was hoping — that the point rider would be the Rurale captain.

But he wasn't. He was a fairly tall man, weathered to the colour of old oak, thin and wearing the distinctive crossed bandoleers across his chest which denoted Mexican irregular soldiers — or maybe outlaws, renegades, just about anyone from below the line that favoured the notion of adding excessive weight in order to cow people more than to kill them.

Bandoleros.

Neither of the men in the rocks knew of any significance to crossed bullet belts worn over the chest. This was in fact the first time they had seen them, and it troubled Jeff a little; the Rurales he had seen before, in fact all the Mexes he'd seen before, had not worn shellbelts across their chests. He was about to mention this to Heber, when one of the wing riders, the man on the east side of the head-hung remuda, yanked to a halt, studied the ground, circled to examine it further, then drew rein peering ahead.

He had found shod-horse tracks of two men riding from the east on an angling course in the direction of those buckskin rocks up ahead.

Jeff eased his head down, slowly snugged the carbine back and curled a finger inside the guard as he tracked the stationary man down his Winchester barrel.

There was no doubt but that wing rider had found the tracks Jeff and Heber had made coming down-country on their southwesterly ride.

Jeff was holding his breath to fire when that wing rider raised his big hat and wig-wagged with it, pointing toward those two motionless men with rifles.

Heber's breath eased out slowly. "He thinks them gents is us."

Jeff eased his curled finger clear of the trigger and hung his head for several seconds; he had come as close as man can come to killing another man. After moments he squinted into the distance. Those two strangers were still out there as though their horses had taken root.

Heber's remark changed a number of things. One was that the horsethieves let the remuda stop, which tired horses would do on any pretext. The second change was that the Mexicans came together to palaver on the east side of the remuda. If they had been concerned about the rocks ahead, their interest was now on those two distant motionless figures.

Heber restated his surmise. "They think them fellers is us."

Whatever the Mexicans thought, their subsequent action was understandable. They got back into place on both sides and behind the remuda, and sent the

134

horses flying with shouts and sixgun fire into the air.

Jeff and Heber watched them take their positions confident they knew what must happen next, and when it happened, they nestled low, tracked two vaqueros and shot almost simultaneously.

Both men were hit, but only one went off his horse. The other one rode bent over, reins loose, evidently solely concerned with remaining in the saddle as his horse ran parallel to the dust-scuffing loose stock.

The result of those gunshots was that the westerly wing rider, who would be close to the rocks if he kept his place, fell back leaving the remuda free to split off, which they did not do — could not do — until they were south of the sandstone boulders.

He dropped back to meet the rider in the drag where the dust was thickest. It was not clear what was happening back there until most of the remuda was passing, and since the horses made more dust than the remuda Jeff and

Heber sprang up to race back for their horses, sprang aboard and raced parallel to the remuda's leaders. It was not an even horse race. Two fresh, rested horses against a herd of tired, sore-footed horses. They passed the leaders and turned back yelling and firing guns. The horses did not stop, they simply turned back causing mass confusion.

Heber and Jeff charged at them. The confusion persisted, clouds of dust rose, but eventually the weary animals were heading north again, not with the haste of other times, but not trotting either.

Heber was easing easterly to prevent a drift in that direction when the gun went off. He looked for the man who had fired it, thought he saw a silhouette in the dust and fired.

The horse went down with both front legs folded under him like a dog. His rider was catapulted ahead and miraculously landed on his feet.

Heber recognised him as the man

recovered from a stumble, swung around and crouched with Heber less than a hundred and fifty feet away with his sixgun riding loose and easy. Heber yelled above the other noises. "You son of a bitch." He levelled the sixgun and squeezed off a shot. Notwithstanding that the hurricane deck of a running horse is one of the worst places to fire from with any expectancy for accuracy, this time the Mexican was too close.

He went spun sideways by impact, fell on his side, tried to roll over and slumped lifeless.

Heber went past with his gun lowered for a final shot. There was no need. He ran past sitting sideways looking back until Jeff's voice rose above the noise of horses. Jeff wig-wagged with his hat and pointed. The remuda was reversing itself with an almost fatalistic resignation. It was streaming northward again.

Heber looked in the direction of Jeff's agitation. Those two distant riflemen were riding to overtake either the drovers or the horses. They evidently had no gun boots, at least for rifles with long barrels, and closed the distance with Winchesters balanced on their hips.

Heber holstered his handgun, kept near the drag of the loose stock where dust was thickest, and watched the oncoming horsemen. They were clearly well-mounted. The distance had been considerable but they were closing in fast.

Jeff left the remuda to cross toward his partner. It was difficult to make Jeff out. As he was getting closer someone fired a gun. The sound was high, more waspish, than either a saddlegun or a sixgun made.

Heber jerked half around in his saddle, grabbed the saddlehorn and dug in his spurs. He probably did not see Jeff as he sped past with flopping reins. Jeff could not see him clearly, but he had ridden with Heber Madden long enough to know he would not flee from a fight. He also had never seen his partner ride leaning over with both hands on the apple.

In a sudden fit of anger Jeff slid to a halt, hit the ground before his horse had stopped, raised his carbine, caught a glimpse of a mounted man southward, and fired. He missed. A mounted rider was hard to hit even without dust obscuring him.

He levered up and fired again. This time the pair of riders turned westward and spurred hard. Jeff levered up for his third shot, but one of the fleeing men fired first. Jeff heard the bullet pass his head. It was sufficient distraction for him to wince as he fired. That time his slug broke a sandstone boulder as though it were a pumpkin. It hadn't even been a near miss.

He did not get another shot. The strangers got among the big rocks and were lost to sight. Jeff mounted his excited animal, spun and went in search of Heber. When he found him, Heber was still atop the horse, which was standing still with both reins on the ground.

Jeff rode close and leaned. They were clear of the dust otherwise he might not have seen the blood. He swore and leaned to touch his partner. Heber spoke without straightening up. "Keep the horses moving. I'll be along."

"The hell with the horses. Where are you hit?"

"In the side, like to knock the breath out of me." Heber released one hand from the saddlehorn and groped. His palm came away scarlet.

Jeff looked back. He could not see them but had no doubt about them still being back there. He leaned, caught a rein and led Heber's horse which, with seven-foot reins, was able to get behind the thoroughbred again. He offered no resistance, which was fortunate. Not all horses could be led well from another horse.

The loose stock was down to a lope but continuing northward. There did not appear to be any break-aways, whatever high spirit those animals had once had, they completely lacked now, which was an ideal way to drive loose horses, except that right at this moment Jeff had other things on his mind.

He kept within the dust as much as he could, and once when he found a gap between tired horses he led Heber's animal to the west side and loped steadily northward, not hastening but still able to pass some of the loose stock.

He did not know the country ahead. Not for many miles would he be in familiar country — that eerie damned burnt hills country. For once he did not dislike the idea of getting back up there. But it was one hell of a long ride.

He loped for two miles then halted allowing the remuda to pass.

Sure as hell those strangers were still back there, but although he waited, squinting for a sighting, as long as the remuda passed there was too much intervening distance and dust.

He resumed his northward ride, thought he saw some trees ahead, which turned out to be some kind of filmy, delicate bush that was called a tree but wasn't one and where Jeff and Heber came from wouldn't even be called a decent bush.

There was no way they could stop without being detected. Widening the distance was the only solution, and it was tenuous the Lord knew.

He was so occupied with his wounded companion and those riflemen back yonder, he only remembered the Mexicans when someone up ahead who had evidently sought cover by riding amid the loose stock, suddenly panicked, burst out of the remuda on the east side and rode low over his animal's neck going due east as hard as he could ride. He never once looked back. Jeff watched as long as the dust did not interfere with the sighting then returned his attention to other things. By his calculation there was one Rurale left. He did not speculate which one it might be, not right at the moment, later he would. Heber could have cleared that up for him, except that the farther north they went the more Heber drooped and clung to the saddlehorn.

Jeff would have to stop soon. Heber would fall off his horse if they went ahead much farther. He looked for some kind of shelter but there was none, not even more of those strong-looking but easily shattered sandstone boulders.

The sun was high and hot. The horses, with dumb instinct, kept trying to veer westerly a little, eventually Jeff let them do it because without jarring hell out of Heber, he could not ride hard enough to turn the leaders.

There were many things about equine intelligence that frustrated riders, but instinct was not one of them. Jeff did not see the spindly water-willows until the remuda increased its tired gait. Then, the greenery appeared.

Jeff was pleased. He let the big

thoroughbred have its head and tugged Heber's horse along. One look at his partner told Jeff all he had to know: He would not be able to go much farther.

The horses flung themselves at the miserly little warm-water creek, their thirst sufficient so that although they crowded, they did not fight as horses normally did when crowded.

Jeff swung off, got Heber down and supported him as far as thin willow shade. He took a moment to hobble their saddle animals, another moment to squint southward, then went into the shade, knelt, considered Heber's injury and brought back two hatsful of creek water to sluice off the blood. Heber seemed to have difficulty breathing. The injury was a wide, ragged tear. Jeff tried to locate the place where the slug entered and failed, mainly because where it had entered, it had skirted just below the skin after ploughing its initial furrow, then had exited where the ribs curved.

Heber was conscious but with his eyes closed. Jeff's ministrations had undoubtedly caused pain but Heber only showed this by an occasional tightening and loosening of his eye lids.

The feeling of helplessness Jeff experienced made him rock back on his heels. He would not leave Heber. On the other hand he instinctively knew that even if he could get him back atop his animal, unless he was securely tied up there he would fall off.

The horses were content to stand in thin shade, drip water, wade out into it, and stand without moving. Those with feverish tender hooves found relief in the water.

Jeff stood up. If those riflemen were coming there was no sign of them. Of the solitary surviving Mexican there was no sign. Neither, gawddammit, was there any sign that Jeff could find help, the land was empty.

He was between a rock and a hard place, a situation he had experienced before, but those other times had not involved a man he thought would die, but he would not leave until that happened, not with those riflemen back yonder.

He did not worry about the Mexican, as hard as he had been riding at Jeff's last sighting of the men, he would be so distant by the time the stalking riflemen came up he would not be a threat.

And they did appear. Riding together with rifles balanced across their laps. They did not see Jeff because of the backgrounding half stunted and scraggle greenery, but he saw them, told Heber he would have to leave him for a while, left his horse but took his Winchester and faded out among the scraggly disorder of that growth which grew on both sides of the creek.

He could see them very clearly with no dust. They were tall men, as alike as two peas in a pod, except that one was older than his companion. They wore clod-hopper lace shoes, the variety of footwear settlers wore. They also wore suspenders and badly wrinkled, faded old trousers. One wore a butternut shirt, the other wore a faded reddish shirt with only two buttons at the gullet, the kind a man had to pull over his head.

Their horses were far more presentable than their riders. They were well-cared for animals, with thick chests, powerful upper forelegs and good heads.

Jeff watched the riders track him, let them ride up and stop gazing down at Heber before he called out.

"Drop the guns — *now!*"

Neither of them seemed startled and neither of them obeyed. Jeff cocked his Winchester, raised it, aimed at the older of the two men. "You son of a bitch, I'll blow your head off! *Drop the guns!*"

The older man turned a weathered, hard expressionless face with pale eyes and a slit of a mouth. He looked steadily at Jeff, spat amber and rested both hands atop the saddlehorn. Everything he did was methodical and evidently without fear. He spoke in an accent which could have come from Texas, or maybe some even more southerly area.

"Mister, we got no use for horse-thieves. In fact of all kinds of life, we got reason to hate them worst of all. Now then, if you figure you can shoot me before Bobbie shoots you, go right ahead an' put it to the test. One way or t'other, horsethief, you're as good as dead."

Jeff stared at the lean, very tall scarecrow on his good-looking horse. "Horsethief? What the hell are you talkin' about?"

"Mister, we seen you'n your friend here lope past our place earlier in the day. We figured you was up to no good so we trailed along, an' sure enough you fellers got into some rocks to intercept that remuda. We seen you shoot two of them drovers an' turn the horses back . . . Thought you'd get clean away didn't you? Thing is, mister, you didn't know us Bartons got a real passion against horsethieves. A real downright passion. We've lynched some now an' again. We — "

"Oh for Chris'sake," Jeff said, lowering the Winchester. "Those were our horses. Those Mexicans was Rurales dressed like vaqueros. They been tryin' to steal our remuda and take it down into Mexico. We'n the army and a feller named Don Alvarez caught 'em a few days back, shot hell out of them, got back our horses, an' that damned Rurale captain caught us again."

The older man said, "Is that a fact? Well now, I know the Alvarez mark when I see it. You stole them horses from him. Mister, you're lucky it's us an' not him caught you. We'll take you down where there's some trees an' leave you hangin' for the birds to peck on. Mister Alvarez — them Messicans got a nasty little trick they play, they turn a man loose to run for it, then shoot him in the back."

149

9

Toward Nightfall

JEFF blew out a ragged breath as he studied the strangers. A man did not have to be gifted to recognise uncompromising individuals when he saw them.

He pointed. "Go look at the left shoulders of them damned horses," he told them. "If you know Alvarez then you know his mark."

Neither of the expressionless tall men raised a rein hand. The older one spat aside. "You stole them horses from Alvarez. He's the only rancher in this country that's got that many to be run off." As Jeff started another protest, the younger of the riflemen raised a hand for silence before he said, "It was clear as day, mister, we seen you two run past headin' west. You had to get into position to intercept them Messicans headin' south. It was as neat a bushwhack as me'n paw ever saw."

The older man rolled his cud from one cheek to the other one before speaking again. "Mister Horsethief, it was your kind that killed my oldest boy when we come onto 'em doin' exactly like you'n your hurt friend was doing. We never let no damned horsethief ride off when we catch 'em. Never have, never will. We'll exterminate every gawddamned lousy horsethief we can find. So far we racked up a respectable count. Now, you want to try'n raise the carbine again, you go right ahead."

They were both facing forward, both rifles in their laps were pointing directly at Jeff. It was too late to wish he'd shot them instead of challenging them.

An unmistakable sound came into the deathly silence. Heber had cocked his sixgun. It was shot-out but he did not know it and the clod-hoppers were too distant to be able to see empty shellholes in the gun's cylinder.

Heber said, "Take their guns, Jeff . . . Either of you so much as cough . . . "

Jeff was leery as he approached the older one first, took the Winchester rifle, dropped it and went toward the second one. Neither of the settlers resisted, they sat their horses gazing at Heber, whose physical activity had started the bleeding again. Heber gave another order. "Get down."

The tall, thin men dismounted with their backs to Jeff. Heber was sweating hard, his hand with the cocked Colt was shaking. He eased the weapon down on his stomach and closed his eyes.

Jeff punched the tall men for hideouts. They had none. The older man gazed at Heber but addressed Jeff who was behind him. "Your friend's goin' to die."

Jeff punched the older man over the kidneys with a sixgun barrel, hard enough to make the other man wince. "Lie face down. If you feel brave give me just half an excuse . . . "

They got belly-down but as Jeff leaned to yank away the older man's belt, he turned his head. "You better stop that bleedin horsethief. If you don't that son of a bitch will die."

Jeff struck the older man over the head, not hard but hard enough. The older man jerked once then went limp.

The other tall man twisted with a snarl. Jeff cocked the man's own sixgun and waited. For three seconds nothing changed. Then the snarling younger man went flat down again.

Jeff did not bother with the unconscious man but he trussed the younger one like a shoat, rolled him face up and glared.

"You dumb pair of sons of bitches," he exclaimed. "What I told you was the gospel truth. Those are our horses, we were gettin' them back from those damned horsethieves. You think I got to lie to you? I could blow your heads off, nothin' you could do about it. Why would I have to lie?"

Heber spoke sounding tired. "Forget 'em, Jeff."

Heber had his eyes open, when Jeff leathered the gun he'd appropriated he went to the creek, got another hatful of water and trickled it.

Heber said, "Thanks . . . How bad is it?"

Jeff lied. "I don't know. Looks like maybe it just skimmed along under your hide an' come out again."

It's not often a man lies and tells the truth with no idea he is telling it.

Heber was revived by cold water. He tried to jockey himself up on both elbows to examine his wound. He might have been able to, but Jeff pushed him down. "Don't move. It only starts the bleedin' again."

They regarded each other, Heber, who was not normally an optimistic soul, made a little grin. "Mister Dixon'll send someone to find us an' shoot us. By now we should've got up there."

Jeff grinned back. "Whoever he sends

better be real good. We got experience. We been cussed out, chased, shot at, snuck up on . . . "

Heber's faint grin lingered. "You ever see such a desolate country before? Hell of a place for a man to die."

"You're not going to die."

Heber's weak smile returned. "You guarantee it?"

The younger man was trying to say something behind his gag. He writhed and thumped the ground with tied feet.

Jeff turned. The man was straining to speak, his eyes bulged, sweat dropped from his chin. He tried to speak with his eyes, he rolled them, looked as far west as he could, and made strangling sounds.

Jeff went over, knelt, removed the gag and sat back. There were no preliminaries. The man raised his body with considerable effort. "They're coming!"

"Who's coming?"

"*Them!*" The man strained half

155

around with his body arching off the ground.

Jeff looked in the direction the man was staring. A bunched-up party of horsemen were approaching without haste. They had the sun in their faces and nothing but rough open country in the direction from which they were riding.

The distance was great but Jeff determined one thing despite that; whoever they were, they weren't Mexicans. He asked who they were. The younger man did not answer the question, he instead said, "Turn me'n paw loose. I'll give you a hunnert dollars."

Jeff considered the distant horsemen and the man whose father had called him Bobbie. "Why would you do that?" he asked Bobbie, and got an almost breathless response. "Look under my shirt. There's a hunnert dollars in one of the flaps of the money-belt. Take it an' set us loose. Hurry up, damn it."

Jeff continued to squat there alternately

watching the agitated man tied at ankles and wrist and those un-hurrying riders steadily, seemingly inexorably riding toward the creek.

Bobbie strained so hard a large vein in the side of his neck swelled. Nearby Heber was still, eyes closed, his blood clotting. His body where he had been wounded was swelling and showing considerable discolouration.

Closer, the elder of the tall men was beginning to show signs of returning consciousness. His companion was begging desperately to be freed. Jeff ignored him as he watched the older man come round, slowly, very slowly, but unmistakably recovering. Jeff watched the older man get unsteadily up onto all fours like a newborn calf. He raised the younger one's sixgun, waited until the older was looking, then cocked it.

As cloudy as the older man's mind had to be, that identifiable and uniquely distinct sound, widened the older man's squinty eyes. The return of his faculties

157

had been hastened. The younger one said, "Look yonder, they're coming."

The older man looked, blinked a few times then faced Jeff as he spoke, "That's a posse, Mister Horsethief. Between me'n my boy we got three hunnert dollars in money-belts. You set us loose right this minute an' you can have all of it."

Jeff eased down the dog, holstered his appropriated weapon and considered the older man. "What do they want you for?"

The old man's narrowed eyes were fixed on the slow-riding but inexorable band of riders. "For robbin' a bank."

Jeff coldly smiled. "A gawddamned outlaw. You'd have shot us, an' you're no better. In fact, you're worse. We aren't wanted by the law."

The older man got into a sitting position, still watching those oncoming riders. "Three hunnert dollars — now! Right damned now! Bobbie, fish out your belt and give him the money."

As Bobbie was doing this with

unsteady hands, his father did the same — with steady hands.

They put the greenbacks on the ground in front of Jeff. Heber spoke. "Take it, Jeff. Anythin' to get rid of them."

Jeff already had the younger man's handgun. After stuffing the money inside his shirt he methodically punched loads out of the older man's belt-gun and tossed it over. He then freed the younger one. Neither of them wasted a second getting to their horses and heading south in a dead run.

Distantly those inexorable riders also turned southward and also gigged their animals into a run.

Jeff watched for a while then faced his partner. "I hope they get caught. Damned bank robbers an' they had the guts to set in judgement on us."

Heber had something different to say. "Help me on my horse, whether them possemen catch 'em or not, one side or the other will eventually come back here. Lend me a hand."

Jeff did no such thing. "You're too puny to make it, Heber. Besides, it's not bleedin' now but the minute you got on a horse it would commence to."

Heber almost scowled. "You want to set here until they come back."

Jeff went over to the creek to splash tepid water over his head and face. He returned with a hatful which he trickled over his wounded partner. Heber endured the abrupt cold and ignored it. "Jeff, no matter which bunch comes back — "

"Shut up, I'm thinking."

Heber didn't shut up. "You go find someone from the Alvarez place, fetch some of them back . . . If them other fellers come back before you return — hell, even someone who got a son killed by horsethieves wouldn't shoot a wounded man on the ground."

Jeff's gaze was sardonic. "You must've been sleeping, or you'd have heard what the old bank robber said. Him an' his boy got a special hatred for

160

horsethieves . . . Hold it; let me finish. I know — we're not horsethieves, but that old man believes we are. If he comes back . . . believe me, Heber, that old screwt'll shoot a man wounded on the ground."

"Go find someone an' fetch 'em back," Heber reiterated as he picked up his sixgun. Jeff looked down, squinted and leaned lower. As he straightened back making a soundless whistle, he said, "That damned gun don't have loads in it, Heber."

The wounded man reversed the gun, looked, and would have punched out spent casings but was so clumsy attempting it Jeff finished the job for him, re-loaded the gun and handed it back.

He got water from the creek for Heber, paid absolutely no attention to the loose stock, removed the hobbles on the thoroughbred horse and delayed leaving for as long as he could. The idea of those tall men returning to find Heber helpless troubled him. Heber guessed why he was fiddling around and said, "Go, damn it."

Jeff rode north. For some miles he let the big horse have its head and lope. The big horse, like most thoroughbreds, had a long, flexible back. It was almost like riding a rocking chair, and the big horse was rested. He paced himself so well that even when Jeff would have hauled him down to a walk, the big horse might have sensed the urgency, but in any case he only walked for a mile or so, then, still on a loose rein, eased over into that rocking-chair lope again.

Jeff tried to recall the fight. He had no difficulty except for small details. He could not remember them very well. Later, years later, he would be able to fit in details, but from how things turned out, not from memory.

The sun moved on its ancient course. When it was in the face of the man on the big horse, Jeff tipped his hat and continued northward right up until he saw several riders converging on him from both sides. This time when he brought the thoroughbred down to a walk the big horse was too interested in the converging horsemen to lope again. He walked along with his big stride.

Jeff identified the riders from a distance as Mexicans. When they too hauled back down to a walk they were close enough for Jeff to recognise the centaur-appearance of one of them. He halted, spat cotton and for the first time in many hours, he smiled.

Tiburcio rode up looking surprised. Before he halted Jess started talking. The other three vaqueros came up and also halted to listen. Before Jeff had finished Tiburcio said something peremptory to a vaquero. The man whirled away and rode northward.

Tiburcio and his companions dismounted. Jeff did too. These were more nearly horsemen than cattlemen. They symbolised the difference. A cowboy was someone who knew a little about cattle and nothing about horses, such as sitting on them for long periods of inactivity.

Tiburcio asked Jeff to describe the bank robbers. When he had done this all three vaqueros smiled but only Tiburcio spoke — for the best of all reasons, his companions did not speak English. The old vaquero said. "We know them. They are bank robbers who also stop stages, but Don Alvarez said years ago, he felt better having neighbours to the south who hated horsethieves." Tiburcio shrugged. "Those possemen won't catch them. That old man knows every coyote den, every big rock from here to the border. Now we should go back and find your partner." At Jeff's faint, frowning look he also said, "Julio, that rider I sent back, will come with a wagon. I told him to put plenty blankets in the back."

As they were turning southward Tiburcio asked questions which Jeff answered. It was a long ride, the last third of it was made with night

164

approaching. During those last miles there was very little talk.

Tiburcio almost imperceptibly leaned his head, first to the right, then to the left. The vaqueros peeled off to the east and west.

The old vaquero produced two very dark, nearly black little crooked cigars. He offered one to Jeff, who declined, lit up the other one, and when the smoke drifted over past the man beside him Jeff coughed, Tiburcio's worn-even teeth showed in a broad smile. He removed the little Mexican cigar, tipped ash, said nothing and rode along with shadows thickening.

Eventually he drew rein, held up his hand, trickled foul-smelling smoke and listened. When he was satisfied they continued southward. Because Jeff was on the vaquero's left side and it was getting dark, he did not see the older man ease his right hand down, pull loose the tie-down thong over his holstered Colt.

They dismounted and led their horses

the last half mile. The gloom was silent until a horse nickered and the big thoroughbred, like most thoroughbreds a genial herd-animal nickered back.

Tiburcio swore softly in Spanish and halted. But the distant nicker from somewhere along that warm-water creek was not repeated, and there was no other sound or a suggestion of movement.

Tiburcio leaned. "You go ahead."

As Jeff swung back astride the vaquero let him get ahead then followed, leading his own horse. He knew one of the simple facts of life. In fact it may have been this knowledge, along with others like it, that had ensured Tiburcio's long life.

If there was an ambush in place where Heber was lying, the bushwhackers would know the man on the long-legged big horse. They would concentrate on him as he rode in.

Bushwhackers were susceptible to reverse ambushes, as long as they had something to watch. Tiburcio left his animal tied to a spindly bush, and removed his spurs. His creeping approach was helped by increasing darkness.

Jeff rode straight up. He made a good target even in poor light.

Nothing happened. He rode to the creek, dismounted, saw Heber lying there, eyes closed, body slack for all the world a dead man.

Jeff knelt and leaned to speak. The sixgun came up with a thumbpad drawing the hammer back. Heber opened his eyes. Jeff pushed the gun aside. "That's the first time I ever come close to gettin' shot by a dead man. Have you got friends out yonder somewhere?"

Heber eased the hammer down, allowed the weight of the sixgun to carry his arm back down, and sighed. "How come you to be back so soon?"

"Tiburcio's out there. He sent a rider back for a wagon."

The old vaquero came forward

without a sound. He was a candid individual. He told Heber he looked like something that had been dug up and resurrected.

Heber put a hand atop his swollen, discoloured body. "I feel like that too. Tiburcio you're a real pleasant sight."

The old man looked around. He was clearly not entirely satisfied there were not enemies in the night. When he faced forward he said, "You need this," and produced a small curved bottle. "Gringo brandy," he explained, and leaned to hand Heber the bottle. He also said, "It burns like fire, the same way fresh *pulque* does."

Heber handed back the bottle with watering eyes. What Tiburcio had said was gospel truth, it burned for a fact. It also got swiftly into the bloodstream. Heber smiled and would have jockeyed up into a sitting position if Jeff hadn't pushed him back down.

Jeff would have liked to have lighted a match to examine the wound, but he didn't, he stood up and rolled a smoke which he lighted inside his hat. Tiburcio wrinkled his nose. *"Gringo cigarillo hebor."*

Jeff looked at the vaquero enquiringly. Tiburcio smiled widely. "I said your cigarette smells nice."

He hadn't said any such thing.

The two vaqueros walked their horses close and sat gazing at Heber. One turned and spoke to Tiburcio, who laughed and gestured to Heber. "Raise your arm. They think you are dead."

Heber dutifully raised his arm. Both vaqueros winced, which made Tiburcio laugh even louder. "If you are dead, how could you do that?" he asked, and answered his own question. "You couldn't, unless you are a ghost, to them a *fantasma*. They are very superstitious."

The vaqueros had scouted and had found nothing. Now they squatted as dark and solemn as carvings watching Heber from a safe distance. Until he, Jeff and Heber spoke among themselves, neither of the vaqueros had said a word. Nor did they after Heber spoke; they made a sign of the Cross.

Night settled, it was warm until Heber and Jeff had been sleeping for several hours, then the cold crept in.

Jeff would have gathered willow faggots for a fire but old Tiburcio wagged a finger at him. The old man had also learned about helping the night remain dark when there was reason to.

10

Always the Horses

IT was a very long wait; the wagon did not arrive until the sun was well up with fresh heat in the day. Tiburcio and his vaqueros had not wasted the time, they scouted as far east as that settler house, and southward. They had only returned from satisfying themselves that neither the bank robbers or their pursuers were in the vicinity when the wagon arrived accompanied by Don Alvarez and three vaqueros. The driver of the wagon was even older than Tiburcio, much darker, incredibly lined. His hair was snow white. He climbed down from the wagon with care. While the others were talking near Heber, this *viejo* produced two croaker sacks fashioned as food bags and cared for the team.

The only time he offered to lend a hand was when the others were carrying Heber to be placed on the straw atop the wagon bed, and since there were already more than enough helpers, Don Alvarez told him in Spanish to water his team without taking them off the pole, while he and the riders rounded up the loose stock.

He had time enough to water ten times as many horses; at first sign of all those mounted men the loose stock, freshened after their long rest, ran in all directions. What kept the horses from making real work of rounding them up was sore feet. When they got the 'crackers' out of their system, they were docile enough to start hiking northward, the only direction they remembered having been driven, and during the course of their travels they watched closely for stones, anything sharp.

It was another long, hot drive, with dust and boredom. For Heber it was not difficult, the old man driving was careful to avoid rocks and rough places.

He sat hunched, concentrating on his work. He did not utter a word all the way back. Neither did Heber unless someone came alongside the wagon to see how he was faring.

Don Alvarez listened to all Jeff had to say and rolled his eyes. He, like Tiburcio, was confident the tall, troublesome bank robbers would not be caught, and although he did not say it, he was beginning to wonder if cowboys from up north were worth their keep. He had now rescued them twice.

But he was pleasant. Even though they had neglected to bring food in their haste, Don Alvarez like his riders, went along without a complaint. Nevertheless they were glad to see the rooftops of their home place.

Several old vaqueros were at the barn to help with the saddle animals. The loose stock was left close by, too close to intermingle with the Alvarez loose animals. The wagon was driven closer to the main-house where for the second time Heber was carefully carried inside and put to bed in that room with no windows.

Jeff stayed with him until he had been fed, then went down to the barn to sleep.

Tiburcio and another vaquero as lean and sinewy but much younger smoked cigars outside on benches and considered the peaceful night. The younger man said, "When we scouted down there we found two dead men." The younger man paused to tip ash. "Do you remember that Rurale they called the Gringo because he grew up in Colorado?"

"Yes. I don't remember his name. He is a Rurale officer."

"Not any more, friend. He was shot and became dead south of where the wounded man was lying. Quite a ways south. He was shot as was another Rurale."

Tiburcio smoked in thought for a while. "In that case Don Alvarez will be pleased."

"And you, *compadre*?"

"Well, I will tell you, those beaners make me very sore where I sit. On the other hand he was a Mexican trying to do what he thought would be right for Mexico, wasn't he?"

The younger inhaled, exhaled, and did not reply for an excellent reason. He had no more use for Rurales than anyone else, and here sat Tiburcio justifying what that man had done.

The younger vaquero arose, nodded and went in the direction of his *jacal*. Tiburcio's old wife came out to sit with her man. Tiburcio was as tough as rawhide, his entire life had been lived hard. He required less sleep. His wife, on the other hand, who lived hard too, was a female. Female women just naturally required more sleep than men.

She told him in Spanish he must come to bed. Tiburcio removed his cigar to consider the length of ash, shook it off, put the cigar back in his mouth and spoke around it. What he said had nothing to do with her comment. "I don't know why gringos up north don't come down here and hire their riders."

"Why should they do that?"

"Because we are better vaqueros. Before we were married Julio's father and I drove four hundred horses along the border for sixty miles without losing a one, without being attacked, without being helped. You don't remember that."

His wife sighed. "No, Tiburcio, I don't remember that . . . But this must be the hundredth time you've told of it. Now come to bed."

The old horseman arose, thought the cigar still had pleasure left in it, so he spat on the end and placed the stub carefully between two faded rooftop slats.

The following day when everyone was rested and had been fed, Jeff borrowed a horse to ride among the Dixon animals. Sore-footed horses could not travel far without being shod. There were too

176

many horses in the remuda for each one to be shod.

They could not be driven all the way to the Dixon ranch in central Colorado either. The only thing left was for the horses to remain in New Mexico until they would be fit to travel again, which meant at least a month and perhaps as long as two months.

Jeff returned to the ranch and went to visit Heber, who had a visitor when Jeff stepped into the doorway. She flashed a look at Jeff and fled from the room. His brief encounter left him with a skimpy impression. She definitely was not one of those sturdy Indian retainers, she was too young and did not weigh within sixty pounds of those other two. He had never seen her before.

Heber nodded toward a chair with a tray and what remained of a meal on plates. Jeff put the tray on the floor sat down and told Heber about the horses. Heber had always been a good listener, only this time as he eased back on a pillow he looked at the ceiling and said, "I expect we got to stay here until they're fit to travel."

Jeff scowled. "If we can't drive 'em, I'd better ride home and explain what's happened down here to Mister Dixon. Hell, we don't want him thinkin' we run off with his horses or his money."

Heber continued to look upward. "Do you know what a *curandera* is?"

Jeff's scowl lingered. "Are you sure you feel all right?"

Heber's gaze came down to his friend's face. "Yep . . . I'll tell you what a *curandera* is. Up north In'ians call 'em medicine women. Down here they're — "

"*Curanderas?*"

Heber raised the blankets to display a new, clean bandage. Jeff leaned and nodded. "She done a good job for a fact."

"Look closer. Come over here. Now then, how much swelling do you see?"

Jeff leaned down, returned to his chair and sat down before replying.

"You're goin' to say some Mex medicine woman did that?"

"Yep."

"How?"

"With some kind of powder. She don't speak much English. But first she washed the wound with what smelt like sage or crushed wild grass, then she cleaned the wound and bandaged it. She smiled. That was when they brought me in here yestiddy. This morning . . . you saw her when you walked in . . . this morning by gawd most of the swellin' an' bad colour was gone. She brought me a special breakfast. I got to admit it didn't taste like ham'n bacon, but Don Alvarez come along an' said it was herbs and whatnot and how did I feel. I told him the truth, I feel fine, weak, mind you, and a little sore, otherwise fine."

Jeff twirled his hat between his knees. He did not believe in medicine-woman healing any more than he believed in ghosts. He stood up to say as long as Heber was going to be laid up at the

Alvarez place for a spell, he'd better ride north to let Mister Dixon know what had happened.

They had been gone long enough to have driven loose stock plumb up to Montana. But Jeff did not saddle up, he first went to talk to Tiburcio, whose unfailing tolerance showed in the way he smiled and explained what curanderas were and how they worked in a land which had never had adequate nor really qualified doctors, and, Tiburcio said with a shrug, he had himself, personally, seen many cures, even what seemed to be miracles, produced by those women.

Jeff said, "Tiburcio, she's too young. Hell, she's no more'n maybe eighteen."

The old man smiled and nodded. "Yes. Very young. Her name is *Pájarita*. She is my granddaughter. She is called Rita."

Jeff was silent so long the old man laughed and changed the subject. "About the horses . . ."

"I'm goin' up north and explain

to Mister Dixon why they can't be moved."

Tiburcio agreed that might be a good idea, but had a question. "Did you talk with Don Alvarez?"

"No. I'm goin' to do that now."

Tiburcio seemed on the verge of speaking again but only nodded as Jeff turned away. He watched the younger man for a while, then went to find shade and light a little cigar.

That was another thing about those people from the north; everything must be done today, maybe even before today. If Mister Dixon had not figured out by now something had happened to prevent his horses from being delivered, he should find out for himself. There was plenty of time. The feed was still strong, there was still water in the creeks. Maybe he was not like other gringos, maybe he would wait as others would do. But as Tiburcio arose to go find his wife and get fed, he doubted that Mister Dixon would be any different from other gringos. They worried, they ran here and there, they yelled and swore, but things happened according to God's will, they could neither be hastened one moment nor delayed one moment, they could only occur if God willed it and when He willed it.

As far as Don Alvarez was concerned, the Dixon horses could remain with his horses until they could travel. Privately he doubted that he would sell horses to gringos from the north again unless they arrived in his yard in strong numbers and heavily armed, took prompt delivery and drove them north without returning for any reason.

Still, what man proposed, God disposed. Don Alvarez was a good host. Much of the time after Jeff had departed, he worked as he had since childhood, as his father and grandfather had worked before him. In the evenings he would visit Heber, whose recovery from the body wound was slow but certain.

They discussed many things over red

wine and tobacco, the way men should. Don Alvarez was not as surprised as Heber was at the way his injury was healing. He would shrug and smile as he said, "A healthy body can take a lot of punishment and still live." He also wondered about Heber and the curandera. Although Don Alvarez was away from the yard most days, those stoic-looking Indian women who moved heavily, almost phlegmatically, and rarely showed expression, were still women who, sometime, years back had been young.

They did not tell Don Alvarez Tiburcio's granddaughter and the gringo spent much time together, and laughed together, they instead wondered aloud in Don Alvarez's presence if Pájarita Reyes and the gringo were not becoming — just possibly — closer than curanderas and patients usually were.

Don Alvarez, a shrewd, knowledgeable individual listened and said nothing. He too had been young. He too had met and laughed with a handsome girl.

He had married her and she had died later in child birth.

Men, being men, Don Alvarez had grieved, never re-married spent all his time supervising his riders and making his holdings profitable, but the image of a laughing girl never left him. In appearance and manner he shared with many other widowers a hard, shrewd, knowledgeable exterior. Inwardly, there was a secret part of Don Alvarez that had survived all those intervening years as fresh as when he had buried the love of his life.

He blessed every child born to his vaqueros. He gave each one a present of money. Later, he would give them a horse, a saddle, and watch stone-faced as they laughed and cried their way toward maturity, never once forgetting that but for the will of God, his child could have lived through the same trials of human existence.

He did not mention Reyes to Heber, who in turn did the same during their evenings together.

They were stockmen, they lived according to the seasons, the blessings of warm rains, the catastrophes of droughts, the curse of rustlers and horse thieves, the cyclical events which, in their particular seasons, followed an ancient routine which was saved from being boring by unexpected accidents, narrowly-averted dangers, and which over lifetimes culminated each autumn with trailing fat cattle to rails-end, after which there came a time of lessened exertion, partly because of winter weather, partly because the sequence of work had particular times to do things which were according to natural law, immutable. Calves could not be altered and branded in driving rain, roundups could not be accomplished through six inches of mud, short days were useless to men whose range covered hundreds of miles.

Only after several days, when Heber was able to walk short distances and he met Don Alvarez out front where a gnarled fig tree grew, and they sat in shade on an old bench, did Heber mention the curandera. Don Alvarez was sweaty, dust layered, tired, he leaned back gazing westerly across land which belonged to him as far as he could see, and farther, his weary mind understanding precisely what was being said and why.

"She's better'n a doctor," Heber said, choosing his words carefully. "Where I come from if I hadn't died by now I'd be settin' on a porch for maybe six months."

Don Alvarez nodded slightly, still gazing far out.

"I got no idea what her medicine is, but it works. That's all that matters, ain't it?"

Again the patrón nodded.

This time silence stretched between them until Heber spoke again. "I expect you'll figure I like her because we been thrown together so much."

Don Alvarez neither moved nor spoke.

Heber sank into another of those

awkward silences. This time he remained quiet so long the patrón's black eyes came around, their gaze was not sceptical, it was curious. Maybe a little sceptical, but mostly curious.

He leaned to arise. He wanted a bath, he was hungry, and most of all he wanted his tumbler of red wine before supper.

He arose, brushed Heber's shoulder with a rough hand and said, "Think long on this, friend. You come from a different world. Pájarita is the apple of old Tiburcio's eye. It would break his heart if you took her away with you — up north where everything would be different to her."

Don Alvarez paused. "Either way, if you took her away or if you stayed down here with her . . . Think hard about it, Heber. You might even talk to Tiburcio."

Don Alvarez walked away leaving Heber sitting in fig-tree shade for as long as was required for shadows to shift and lengthen.

11

A Meeting

FOR Jeff the ride north followed a familiar way until he topped out above Raton Pass. Up there the rearward view was veiled with a light heat-haze, but he knew what lay farther than he could see.

It was cooler on the high plateau. His second and third days of riding he saw only wild animals, no men, no cattle, no horses.

He came to stands of forest interspersed with level to rolling grasslands. He passed places where he and Heber had camped on their way south.

Once, as he was muddying a small creek to reach the far shore, and before he emerged beyond the shadowy willows, he saw two Indians riding eastward. They would cross his path half a mile ahead.

He dismounted, put fingers on the thoroughbred's nostrils and was ready when the animal would have nickered.

The Indians were attired both in buckskin and broadcloth. One wore a headband, the other a rangeman's hat. As nearly as Jeff could make out they were harmless, at least he could not see saddle boots for carbines. What he also could not determine at that distance was shellbelts and holstered pistols.

He rested for a half hour, until the Indians were out of sight, before emerging from the willows and continuing his ride.

His estimate was that it would require a week of riding to reach his employer's ranch. It had taken that long reaching the Alvarez place on the ride southward.

He saw smoke rising from a log house a fair distance west where outbuildings and pole corrals indicated someone ran livestock.

Another time he did something few men ever did, he started up a band of antelope. They neither detected his scent or saw him until he came over a low rise. He saw them at the same time they raised their flags to disclose white rear-ends, and ran so swiftly that within minutes they were lost in a stand of trees.

It was a pleasant ride. Compared to the riding he and his partner had done lately, this trip north was a genuine pleasure.

He did not hurry. Tiburcio would have approved of the reason, which was simply that at last he was heading in the right direction, and another few days would not make much difference in comparison to the length of time he and Heber had been away.

The weather held, nights were cold but days were golden, soft-scented and benignly warm. He and the big thoroughbred had an opportunity to know, to understand, each other in the only way a horseman gets to know a mount, by riding without haste, without demands being made, in good weather with abundant feed and water.

He was about half the distance to be covered when he saw riders approaching from the north. Because of the distance all he felt sure of was that they were not Mexicans.

A solitary horseman in a land where the law arrived at most meetings on a man's hip, it was prudent to avoid contact unless, or until, there was reason to believe those oncoming horsemen were not outlaws, or perhaps lawless individuals who, while they would not rob a bank or stop a stage, nevertheless might succumb to admiration for a solitary rider's horse or money.

Jeff's difficulty was they had seen him at about the same time he saw them. He was in open country. The nearest timber was about a mile distant easterly. If he jumped his horse out to reach cover, the band of riders would probably race in pursuit, if for no other reason than to catch someone who had fled at sight of them, perhaps a renegade with a bounty on his head.

He rode on a loose rein, the big horse, always interested and gregarious, raised his head and nickered. Jeff understood; horses only knew they would be used, they had no capacity to determine whether the two-legged creatures who rode them meant harm to each other or to themselves.

For Jeff, watching the oncoming riders, bunched up so that he had to count them three times before arriving at a correct determination of their numbers, his best, in fact his only course, was ride directly to a meeting.

The horsemen also rode on a loose rein. There were four of them so they had little to fear. Riding without haste gave them the opportunity to assess the man coming north, but for a long time distance precluded a real opportunity to make judgment.

Only when Jeff drew rein, looped his reins and rolled a smoke, did anything happen. The riders halted, milled for a few moments, then resumed their approach. They had made their judgment. When they were less than a hundred and fifty yards distant the lead rider, a large, thick man, stood in his stirrups and called ahead.

"Where the hell you been, where's Heber an' the horses?"

Jeff swung to the ground, smoked and waited until he would not have to yell. As the riders came up he smiled, dropped the smoke and ground it out.

The big man was Harold Dixon, the riders were men Jeff had ridden with, knew very well, and while they did not call a greeting, they dismounted to lead their horses the last few yards, in the wake of the big, bull-necked greying man, who had set the example when he dismounted.

Dixon looked from Jeff to the big thoroughbred and back. He did not look pleased but at least when he spoke he was circumspect. "Where's Heber?

You fellers should have been back ten days ago."

Jeff hunkered in horse-shade and started from the beginning. Before he had completed his tale all the men were also squatting in horse-shade except Harold Dixon. From a squatting position looking upward, Dixon seemed much larger and heavier than he was.

He eventually hunkered with the others. "Don Alvarez's got the horses on his range — safe an' sound?"

Jeff's reply was typical for a horseman. "Safe, Mister Dixon, but I don't know how sound. Like I said, they're too tender-footed to be driven. Their feet are worn to the quick from all that see-sawing back and forth. My guess is that they won't be fit to be drove for another month, maybe longer."

Dixon threw up his arms and rolled his eyes heavenward. But at least for one thing he was grateful; the horses he had bought were safe, neither they nor the money he had entrusted to Forman and Madden had disappeared.

One of the riders grunted up to his feet squinting eastward. Jeff also arose and turned. It was two mounted Indians crossing from east to west. Jeff would have bet his spurs it was the same pair he had seen earlier.

The Indians had seen the gathering of men and horses half a mile or so southward, but they cleared the trees and rode westerly without haste and, at least as nearly as Dixon or his riders could determine without fear.

Dixon softly said, "What are they up to?"

No one answered, they were all wondering the same thing. A thin, greying man with skin the colour of old leather and nearly as creased and wrinkled quietly said, "We could collar 'em."

Harold Dixon did not even consider the suggestion. He had been riding three days to find horses or the men he had detailed to bring north. That was all he'd been thinking about since leaving his home-place to find answers. Two Indians riding cross-country, evidently minding their own business, did not interest him.

He cocked his head to consider the position of the sun, turned to tighten his cinch and mount as he said, "We got maybe three hours daylight left. Let's use it."

As the party rode southward those two distant Indians stopped to watch. They were the same pair Jeff had seen before; they were not Reservation broncos, they were professional horse-thieves. They had been successful at their trade for several years. The fact that they were not strong-hearts, but pragmatic men who had learned from the whites that screaming and charging other men who out-numbered them inevitably led to the grave, their interest in the Dixon riders was professional.

The ride back was comfortable, pleasant because this time Jeff had companions, but every circle of burnt stones, every horse-cribbed tree, every place, such as the one where the *sopilotes* had hovered and where only a few stripped bones remained to mark the fight in the burnt timber country, resurrected memories, most of which were not particularly pleasant.

Mister Dixon was interested in his horses. Jeff told him all he knew about them, which was not a whole lot, there were too many to be remembered individually. He was of the opinion that Mister Dixon had got his money's worth, and that seemed to satisfy the big man.

They made three camps, along toward late afternoon of the fourth day they had rooftops in sight. Mister Dixon said they would camp where they were, near a little warm-water creek amid fire-blackened dead trees. It was a place Jeff would have not selected, but he said nothing.

Mister Dixon took an all-over bath in the creek as did Jeff and another man whose name was Walt Strong, the other men sat with their backs against saddles, smoking or chewing and watching the little supper fire.

Coyotes sounded in the night. Mister Dixon sat up in his soogans with a sixgun in his fist. The rider named Strong murmured from the nearby darkness. "Them In'ians, you reckon?"

Dixon was waiting for more soundings and did not reply immediately, when he did answer his tone of voice indicated he was troubled; after all Jeff had told him, he had little difficulty in perceiving those calls in the darkness as signals between either cut-throats or horsethieves.

Walt Strong roused Jeff, who was the only man among them who knew this burnt timber country. They left Mister Dixon sitting in his underwear with the gun in his hand. Jeff had not heard the coyotes. Lately the sleep that had eluded him earlier, did not elude him now.

He and Walter Strong separated as they moved like dark wraiths over grassy footing that muffled all sound.

A coyote sounded close by but southward. He was answered by the second coyote over eastward on the far side of the encampment.

Where Jeff and Walt Strong came together, Strong said, "Them ain't coyotes, partner. Coyotes don't split off, they run in a pack an' stay in a pack . . . Jeff, you remember them Indians?"

Jeff nodded. They would be unable to find the Indians but they could get close to the hobbled horses and wait. Whoever was out there, if indeed it wasn't four-legged coyotes, would only be after their horses.

As they got among the animals crouching close Jeff said, "This is the gawddamndest country for horsethieves I ever heard of."

Walt Strong was a chewer, he got a tidy cud tucked into his cheek before drawling a reply. "Partner, you never been down in Old Messico, them folks would shoot a man from ambush for his horse, maybe just for his boots and pants and his guns."

Jeff did not respond. His big friendly thoroughbred had raised his head and was standing perfectly still looking westward, behind Jeff and Walter Strong. Jeff nudged his companion, both men got very slowly down against the ground where grass growing hock-high hid them.

They waited. The next time a coyote sounded it was northward. Walt Strong leaned to whisper. "He's come clean aroun' the camp, west to south, south to north, and if he yelps again he'll be over where his friend is westerly . . . What kind of In'ians they got down here?"

Jeff did not respond. Right at this moment he would not have answered if he'd known the answer, which he did not. He dried a sweaty palm on the flattened grass, re-gripped his sixgun and strained to see movement.

Now, all the horses were standing motionless, head-high, watchful, tensed for flight although a hobbled horse has one hell of a handicap. Some, older, savvy animals, can hop faster than a man can run.

If there was such a horse in the Dixon band, Jeff and Walt Strong were not to discover it, at least on this particular night.

Without warning someone fired two rapid shots from the direction of the camp. They had been close enough to sound like one continuing muzzleblast.

Neither Strong nor Jeff looked rearward although both wanted to in the worst way. If whoever had fired those shots had seen the northerly 'coyote' Jeff and Walt Strong wanted to know what the other one was going to do.

They never found out.

An hour later Harold Dixon walked out with the other riders. Dixon had re-loaded his pistol and had it riding where it belonged on his right hip. He said, "That son of a bitch won't be back. I couldn't see him real well, so I aimed where I glimpsed him, then fired a mite westerly where I figured he'd jump if the first shot didn't hit him."

A long silence ensued, eventually broken by Walt Strong. "Well . . . did you hit him?"

Dixon shook his head. "I don't think so, but I had a glimpse of a man jumping higher'n a jack rabbit an' running westerly as hard as he could."

There was no laughter but the men smiled as they headed back for their blankets, all but Jeff who said he would nighthawk in case the 'coyotes' came back, which no one believed would happen, and which did not happen.

In the morning after striking camp with the Alvarez yard in sight, they sashayed until they found barefoot horse tracks where two animals had been tethered, and more tracks showing how bare hooves had dug into the ground toe-first the way running horses did. They followed the sign for about a mile then turned back.

Those 'coyotes' would be miles off and probably still fleeing, unless Mister

Dixon had winged one, then they would probably only go as far as the injured man could ride.

No one mentioned why they did not track for blood. Mister Dixon was down here for his horses, not wounded tomahawks. There was another reason they did not follow up on the pursuit.

Two renegade Indians, one wounded and holed up, would be more dangerous than a den of rattlesnakes.

They watched the Alvarez yard as they rode toward it. They were seen, of course. Jeff watched a lean, sinewy man cross to the main-house and smiled to himself. Old Tiburcio always seemed to be where things happened.

Vaqueros were lounging in front of the barn as the gringos rode in. Black-eyed youngsters peeked, old men angled around so they could also see, even a few women succumbed to curiosity.

Gringos were not a novelty, but a large band of heavily armed riders were a novelty, regardless of the size of their saddlehorns or their hats.

12

A Dying Man

DON ALVAREZ, who had only met Harold Dixon once before was not entirely surprised to see him; it had been his opinion for some time that the gringo rancher should have come himself to take delivery of the horses, but Don Alvarez was the epitome of hospitality. He had Tiburcio show Dixon's riders where they could bed down, took Dixon to the main-house for wine and some conversation, on Dixon's part to relate the brush with the 'coyotes' after which Don Alvarez left Mister Dixon with Heber.

Heber was really surprised to see his employer. Dixon knew Heber had been wounded, Jeff had told him, but when he took the bedside chair for a palaver, he had only a cursory idea of the nature of Heber's injury.

After Heber's personal mishap had been discussed between them, Dixon told Heber, tender footed or not, he intended to take the horses within the next day or two.

Heber, who was not favourable, nevertheless conceded that if the remuda was allowed all the time it needed, while that might entail more delay than Mister Dixon would like, he could make the drive. Tender-footed horses were not cripples, they could be driven, but very slowly and with long periods of rest.

Across the yard Tiburcio and Jeff sat out front of the vaquero's adobe house. It was beginning to appear to Tiburcio that some perverse destiny intended to keep Heber and Jeff in the area, for whatever reason would motivate such a design.

He listened to Jeff's recounting of the encounter with the two Indians, and the old man tipped ash off his foul-smelling little Mexican cigar and blandly said, "Yes. Their names are Matador and Chingadero. They started out stealing horses from the army, an easy thing to do. They kept on doing it after the army left. It is how they make a living."

Jeff stared. The old man's expression remained bland. "You let In'ian horsethieves operate in Don Alvarez's country?"

Tiburcio put his bland look on the younger man, "In this territory, friend, different races of people have been washing back and forth like waves of the ocean. After a time it became clear, as with your men with long rifles where Heber was shot, Indians who steal horses will continue to steal them. Don Alvarez' grandfather and great-grandfather, did what became custom. It started even before the soldiers arrived. The ranchers traded with the Indians — if they did not steal our animals, we would protect them from soldiers and gringo law. It

206

has worked very well for a very long time."

Tiburcio smiled at Jeff. "Those long-rifle men — Don Alvarez has the same agreement with them. They do not steal our livestock nor rob us, and we will warn them against posses, and give what other kinds of assistance we can."

Tiburcio watched Jeff's face for a moment, then softly laughed. "Yes, I know. Up north you ride them down and hang them. We ride them down too, when they violate their promise, which very few have done, and we catch and kill them. But this part of the nation has too many different kinds of people to be killing someone all the time. It would take too much time."

Jeff leaned back. He had to ponder about this arrangement. For a fact, where he came from it would not work, but the fact that it worked down here . . . He shrugged like a Mexican.

The observant and shrewd old vaquero chuckled, finished his cigar and watched

Jeff walk in the direction of the *jacal* where the Dixon riders were to stay.

The following morning Don Alvarez and Tiburcio rode out with the gringos to look at the horses. They were not in as good flesh as they had been but they were in good enough shape. Some were more 'gimpy' than others, but all that signified was that not all horses got tender at the same rate.

Because these animals had been driven first one way then another way so often lately, they did not flee at sight of mounted men, but watched the horsemen with curiosity. After the riders passed the horses went back to grazing.

Heber had wanted to ride with the others. He had even gotten out of bed to dress himself. The curandera blocked the doorway and shook her head. Heber stood indecisively for a moment, then kicked out of his boots.

Pájarita Reyes had brought food which she placed on his lap when he was back in bed. He considered the food for which he felt no need at the moment, and without looking up asked if her name had significance. It had, a *pájarita* was a little bird. When she had been a child Tiburcio had given her that name to tease her, and it had become her actual name.

She also told him something that shocked him. Tiburcio was the son of Don Alvarez's grandfather and an Indian woman named Maria Reyes.

Where Heber, like Jeff, had come from, something like that would never be mentioned. Illegitimacy was an unforgivable sin for the mother, the father, and even for their offspring, the latter of which were held in Mexican eyes to be blameless and therefore not to be scorned nor discriminated against. Such things, as with just about everything else in life, was the will of God. No one would think of berating God. Not if they expected to remain healthy.

She laughed at Heber's expression, sat on the bedside chair and asked questions. Where had Heber been born? Where was his family? How old was he and because it would probably kill him if he rode away with the others in a day or two, why did he not remain where he was until full recovery which, she said with a perfectly straight face might take as long as a year.

He answered her questions before easing back against rolled blankets which served as pillows, and regarded her solemnly for a long time before saying, "You told me last week I was healing very well."

She shrugged. "You are. But riding a horse would open the wounds. You could bleed to death before they could find someone to care for you." Her colour heightened a little but she did not take her eyes off his face.

He returned her gaze as he slowly said, "You wouldn't be telling me this so that I would have to stay, are you?"

Her eyes danced as she arose from the chair. "*Quien es?* Now rest and I will be back later."

Heber gazed at the doorway after she had departed.

Jeff came visiting later in the day. He watched Heber shaving himself using a polished steel mirror in one hand and a razor in the other hand. Heber irritably held out the mirror. "Hold this damned thing, will you? It's hard to shave one-handed."

Jeff held the mirror, told Heber they would be heading north with the remuda tomorrow, and at the scowl of surprise this statement elicited, Jeff also said, "They can travel, not fast; it'll maybe take us a full month to get them up north, but Mister Dixon told me he'd rather poke along an' waste a month, than set around down here for the same length of time with nothin' to do — then start the drive. He's impatient to get back."

Heber used a damp towel to wipe his face and spoke as he was using the cloth. "He's always impatient. Ever since I went to work for him, he's been like that."

Jeff smiled slightly. "Gringos are like that — no?"

Heber finished shaving and leaned back against the rolled blankets. "You're gettin' to sound like the folks down here."

"Don Alvarez told me if Mister Dixon didn't need me, he'd hire me on." As he said that Jeff smiled.

"What did Mister Dixon say to that?"

"I didn't tell him. I'll go north with the remuda . . . "

"Heber, I heard a rumour . . . "

"What rumour?"

"That you'n old Tiburcio's granddaughter, the medicine woman or whatever they call her — is maybe sweet on each other."

Heber could not control the colour that came into his face, nor did he respond to his partner's statement. He said something else. "I'd like to go back with you fellers."

Jeff sighed. "Can you do it? That's an ugly wound you got."

"The medicine woman says I can't."

Again Jeff hung fire before speaking. "I never put much store by them."

Heber answered that quickly. "I do. This one anyway. She patched me real fast."

Jeff arose and put on his hat, considered his partner for a moment before nodding and leaving the room.

Harold Dixon was eating with some unmarried vaqueros at a cooking pit when Jeff came up and sat down beside him.

Sucked his fingers before speaking. "They sure know how to cook meat. It's some kind of sort of sweet, bitter sauce they use." He finished drying his fingers with a bandanna and studied Jeff for a moment. "Heber's went and busted his wound open?"

"No. He wants to go back with us."

"Can he stand the trip?"

"The medicine woman who's been lookin' after him says he can't."

Mister Dixon considered the fragrant

meat on its grate over the cooking pit. The vaqueros spoke little and ignored the gringos. They were hungry men.

"Maybe he'd best stay here until he's able to ride," Mister Dixon said. "I talked to Don Alvarez . . . He told me Heber's welcome to stay as long as he likes. He also told me something else."

"About Heber an' the medicine woman?"

"Yes . . . Did you know about it?"

For a moment Jeff said nothing. One of the vaqueros pitched a rib bone to a nearby dog and precipitated a dog fight. The vaquero swore and got to his feet. The dogs knew when a kick was coming. All fled except the one he had thrown the bone to.

When the furor died Jeff answered Dixon's question. "I didn't know about it but I sort of suspicioned it."

Mister Dixon re-filled his tin cup with hot coffee before he resumed his seat to speak again. "Heber's a good man. Always has been since he went to work for me. I'd sort of dislike losing him." Dixon sipped hot coffee before putting a shrewd glance on his companion. "Jeff, I'm older'n you; I don't think there's a job in the world that could hold a man back if he gets fond of a woman."

About an hour later with thin shadows firming up along the east side of buildings, Tiburcio sought Don Alvarez.

He found him on the bench against the old fig tree, sat down with a troubled sigh and mopped sweat off his mahogany face.

"They told you about the Indian horsethieves, patrón?"

Don Alvarez nodded with a faint frown. "Yes. Why?"

"Because Matador is in my house. Chingadaro brought him. He told my wife one of the gringos shot Matador."

Don Alvarez was silent a long time. The gringos were his guests, the Indians were his allies. He asked if the curandera was with the wounded

Indian. Tiburcio nodded. "She is. So is my wife."

"How bad was he shot?"

"That's why I came for you."

Don Alvarez arose from the bench. "Keep the gringos away from your house. Use any excuse you must. Mister Dixon seems to me to be one who uses his rope for other things than catching calves."

They parted in the yard, Tiburcio toward the place where the gringo riders had been housed, his employer over among the *chozas* of the vaqueros.

The interior of Tiburcio's home had one small window set deeply into the three-feet thick mud wall. Because not even people of substance had glass windows very often, what light entered Tiburcio's house came through a square of rawhide that had been scraped to almost paper thinness. Sunlight came through.

Pájarita and Tiburcio's wife, a very dark woman whose age could have been somewhere between forty and

216

sixty, and who actually was in her mid-seventies, looked up as the patrón entered. They made way for him beside the pallet on the floor where a squatly, very dark Indian was lying in clothing that had both fresh and dried blood on it.

Don Alvarez spoke briefly with the curandera before she disappeared in the direction of the main house for whiskey.

He knelt, returned the feeble smile of the wounded man, leaned to consider the wound, sat back and asked how it had happened.

The Indian, like many in his part of the country, spoke his native tongue as well as Spanish, but no English. The conversation was in Spanish, with a sprinkling of a different language, one that occasionally had guttural sounds.

He said that he and his friend had been shot at for no reason by the white-eyes. Don Alvarez had reason to be sceptical. He had heard Mister Dixon's version of what had happened.

He examined the injury. It had bled a lot. The flesh was swollen and discoloured. The bullet had struck the Indian high on his right side, as though he had been moving when he was struck. Like Heber's wound, the bullet had ploughed beneath the skin and had exited after following around one rib, perhaps two ribs. The entry-hole was clean but the exit hole was large and ragged.

By the time the curandera returned with whiskey Don Alvarez and Tiburcio's wife had finished bathing the wound. Beyond doing those things they had to wait. When the curandera arrived and passed the bottle to the patrón, the Indian's stoicism was wearing thin. He was in considerable pain. Not only had he been shot but he also had two broken ribs.

While the women worked on the Indian Don Alvarez went to the doorway. There were some children playing, otherwise even his own riders were nowhere in sight.

As he turned back Pájarita spoke to him in English. "If Matador had brought him the day he was shot . . . " She shrugged. "There is fever in the wound."

Don Alvarez returned and knelt to smile at the Indian. He held up the bottle. The Indian took three big swallows then fell back on the pallet, eyes tightly closed, mouth open. That whiskey burned all the way down.

The Indian was sweating. His clothing was soaked through. Don Alvarez left Tiburcio's wife, took the curandera and went just beyond the doorway to ask bluntly if the Indian would live.

Just as bluntly she told him that he would not live without a miracle. She put her head slightly to one side and asked her own question. "Does his friend know the gringo who shot this one is here in the yard?"

Don Alvarez eyed the girl with paternal interest. He had seen her grow from infanthood to her present age. She had earned his respect over

219

the years in many ways. "I don't know, but he may not know if he spent the time caring for this one. But of course now that he is no longer burdened he may back-track." Don Alvarez made a wintry smile. "They never forget."

Pájarita mentioned what had occurred to her since the wounded Indian had arrived. "What can you do, patrón? You are between the *Indio* and the gringos."

He shrugged. "Nothing. It will be up to the Indian. The gringos will leave with the horses in the morning. Once they are gone . . . " He shrugged again.

Pájarita returned to the pallet where the perspiring Indian was being fed water by Tiburcio's wife. As he lay back, breathing in broken gasps, the older woman sat back on her heels and wagged her head.

Pájarita felt for fever, which she found, and leaned down because of poor lighting, and slowly rocked back without completing her close examination. The smell told her all she had to know.

She and the older woman went outside where Pájarita told her companion exactly what she had told the patrón; this man was going to die.

The older woman said nothing, she turned to re-enter the house and await the arrival of her husband, who did not arrive until long after Pájarita had knelt, head bowed, to ask forgiveness for all the Indian's sins, to plead that his soul would arise to heaven.

When her grandfather came in, the curandera left. Old Tiburcio, who knew little of cures but who knew a lot about death, stood above the pallet. His wife watched as he stood, expressionless and troubled, fully aware of what would happen over the next few hours.

He left the *jacal* to cross toward the main-house for a palaver with Don Alvarez. The patrón took Tiburcio to the bench near the fig tree, sat down and said, "I told Señor Dixon what has happened, that the other one will know sooner or later, and that I thought the best thing for him to do is start the drive north about sundown. Even tender footed horses can run in an emergency. He may lose a few in the night, but if he doesn't leave right away, when Chingadero is figuring things out, the Indian may stalk them in the night. He will need a gringo to pay for his dying friend."

Tiburcio considered. If he hadn't been as old and experienced as he was he might have suggested that Chingadero did not know his friend would die, but he said no such thing; Indians knew as much about the approach of death as anyone did, maybe more, they had been dying for centuries as a result of lead-bullet wounds.

Tiburcio left his patrón. Don Alvarez sought out big Harold Dixon to explain the situation. Dixon listened, showed initial surprise, then showed nothing at all as he said he would get the men, have the remuda brought closer in and as soon as visibility diminished, he would do exactly as Don Alvarez said, and if he lost a few horses that would be a price he would be glad to pay to get his remuda and his riders away from the burnt timber country.

Jeff heard the plan while he and Walt Strong were sipping red wine from tin cups. That wiry little grinning ape of a vaquero who had a smattering of English and who had become almost Jeff Forman's shadow, had furnished the wine.

Jeff groaned, Walt Strong, a laconic individual, did not like the idea of driving sore-footed horses, particularly through darkness, but if red wine did nothing else, its capacity for overcoming dislikes was unsurpassed.

They parted, Strong to find the other Dixon riders and explain what was to occur, while Jeff went over to the main-house to tell Heber they would have to leave him behind.

He anticipated dismay and resentment,

instead he found Heber leaning on his rolled pillow-blanket staring at the ceiling while wearing an expression Jeff could not have defined. He had never seen that look on his partner's face before.

Jeff launched into his explanation while leaning in the doorway. Heber heard him out before saying, "Every trail has a fork, Jeff."

The man in the doorway looked puzzled. "What does that mean?" he asked.

"Maybe next summer, or the summer after you could ride down here. It'll be like old times, partner."

They looked steadily at one another for half a minute without either of them speaking before Jeff smiled, nodded, and departed.

The dissolution of a partnership which had endured for several years left a man with a small pain of loss, but as Heber had said, every trail had a fork.

13

One More Try

TIBURCIO sent two vaqueros to see where Chingadero had gone. They could only track the Indian as long as daylight lasted. The Indian had gone northwest and when the vaqueros turned back, they were convinced that the *Indio* had some distant objective.

Tiburcio breathed a prayer about that even though he thought he knew where Chingadero was going — to the *rancheria* of his people to recruit warriors before returning.

Tiburcio said nothing to any of the gringos or to Don Alvarez. He could have used the excuse that there was too much dust and noise. His guess did not have to be correct anyway.

The horses were turned northward

225

with Walt Strong riding point. Like cattle, horses would follow a leader, without a leader they had to be driven.

The sun was reddening, which made the dust rust coloured. It had been a hot day. The heat would linger even after sundown. Tiburcio, along with others and Don Alvarez listened as the shouts grew fainter, then turned back to their own concerns. Only once Don Alvarez rolled his eyes skyward. He had sold hundreds of horses, to the army, to Mexicans, to freighters and stockmen; never before had he been so plagued with difficulties getting the damned things on their way, and, hopefully this time, staying on their way.

Harold Dixon was equally as forceful in his thoughts. He had bought — and sold — horses for many years; never had he experienced as much trouble with a remuda as he'd had with this one. And it was exasperating too that the pace had to be set to the slowest of the herd. As those who knew Harold Dixon knew, he was a hard-driving man to whom delays were anathema.

At least this time regardless of his will and wish there was nothing he could do about a situation which was beyond his — or anyone else's — control.

There was time to talk. Driving tired, tender animals was not the customary keeping horses in sight, but rather easing the drag along as though the horses were cattle.

Walt Strong brought up the drag with Jeff Forman. Walt did not use the customary bandanna to shield his face from dust. He studied the horses, chewed, occasionally expectorated and leaned to address Jeff in his laconic way. "If the old man give more'n fifteen dollars a head for this bunch he got skinned."

Jeff was thinking of Heber back yonder; he was speculating on the whims of fate. Heber might hitch harness with the curandera, in which case it was likely he and Jeff would never meet again because, as far as Jeff Forman was concerned, if he never saw the burnt timber country again he would not feel badly.

Mister Dixon dropped back. The point rider far ahead was slouching along with one foot out of the stirrup. He was one of those damned fools who had *tapaderas*, not the sensible monkey-face variety, but the twenty-one inch Eagle Bill kind, which, being heavy, swung slightly back and forth so that at the end of the day when a man dismounted unless he had ankles of iron, they either folded under him or at least wobbled.

Mister Dixon asked about the curandera. Jeff told him all he knew. She was very pretty, about five or six years younger than Heber, and — for a woman — pretty savvy about things.

Mister Dixon pondered for a few yards before asking another question. "What kind of In'ians was them two — one of which I shot?"

Jeff had no idea, but Indians were Indians. He said, "Whatever kind he is, I wouldn't bet a plugged *centavo* he'll take it sittin' down when the other one dies."

Walt Strong nodded about that but said nothing. Mister Dixon stood in the stirrups to look back. There was no movement except dust. He settled forward. "What the hell happened to them trees? Must have been a bad fire to cook so many of them."

When they passed along the ridge above the place where the disguised Rurales had been killed, Jeff pointed out the area and told Mister Dixon what had happened, and that threw the big man into another long silence.

They were well along before daylight began to fade, and even farther before dusk finally shortened visibility, but did not immediately ameliorate the heat.

When they arrived at a warm-water creek some horses drank thirstily while others, the ones with feverish feet, waded in, then drank.

The point rider came back to say he'd seen a horseman up ahead. Mister Dixon scowled. "How far ahead?"

The point rider pointed. "Hard to say with night comin' an' all. I'd guess may be half a mile or so."

Dixon sent the point rider and a companion back to see if they could find the horseman. After they had departed he spat, looked around at this haunted place of dead trees and little else, mopped sweat off his face and exasperatedly stowed the bandanna as he looked at Jeff Forman. He seemed ready to speak then changed his mind and went on foot closer to the creek where tanked-up, tired and sore-footed horses paid him slight heed.

Walt Strong looked disgusted. "Well, are we goin' to set up here for the night or not?"

Jeff did not reply. He watched the riders watering their horses, took his own animal over for the same purpose, and Mister Dixon gruffly said, "When them boys get back we'll move out. As long as we got any kind of light I'd like to keep going."

As far as Jeff was concerned, he

approved, but the remuda really had come far enough for the shape it was in.

When the drive was continued the horses now, among their other problems, had guts full of water which tended to make them even more sluggish.

Mister Dixon kept to the drive even as dusk faded into darkness. The horses knew the route, but they were now travelling on 'bottom' alone. Jeff rode up where his employer was and told Mister Dixon there was another of those piddling little warm-water creeks about a mile ahead. Dixon did nothing more than nod his head.

Jeff dropped back where tired horses were becoming more of a problem for the drag riders. Walt Strong reined up when he came close, spat and said, "What's he figurin' to do, lose half his damned horses in the night?"

Jeff had no comment about that either. He — and Walt Strong — got paid for doing what Mister Dixon wanted done.

When they finally halted for the night that measly little creek made the trail at least bearable, but after the remuda tanked up the horses did not do as horses normally would do, they did not fan out a little to graze or browse depending on the kind of available feed, they stood in creek-mud with water dripping, and seemed disinclined to move now that they had water and could rest.

Mister Dixon said they would make a dry-camp, which his riders, already disgruntled, bleakly accepted as they went about digging in saddlebags for food. To drink they had to hike eastward a fair distance before finding un-muddied water.

Jeff shed his boots, hat and heavy shellbelt. He lit a smoke inside his hat and leaned back to consider a flawless sky with its lop-sided moon.

He got along well with Mister Dixon, but there were times when a man just had to move on, something like his present condition encouraged those kinds of thoughts.

Nothing had gone right since he and Heber had arrived in the burnt timber country, and it still was not going right.

He heard a coyote sound. With one motion he killed the smoke and reached for his boots. None of the other drowsing men heeded a sound as familiar to them as rain.

Jeff waited for the second call. This time, there was no second call, and that squared with his suspicion that the surviving horsethief had not gone all the way to his rancheria for reinforcements. He had gone out far enough to parallel the drive, then he had remained even with it out of sight.

Jeff frowned. Why would Chingadero make his coyote call if he was alone?

Maybe it had been a genuine coyote. An experienced Indian could fool anyone. Jeff slowly swung his shellbelt into place and buckled it. Maybe. But it was better to be safe rather than sorry. Whichever it was, a coyote or a tomahawk, being prepared was not a bad idea.

He did not mention his suspicion to the others, they were tired, even Mister Dixon was slumped against the ground.

It was in Jeff's favour that tired horses with sore feet and full bellies might cock an eye as he moved like a wraith among them but did not shy.

It still bothered him that if an Indian had imitated a coyote, why would he do it if he were alone? He wouldn't, which meant there could be more than one out there. However, since there had been no acknowledging reply this did not have to be true.

He sought without success to find horses with their heads up. He moved slowly, carefully, attuned to everything but particularly to movement.

There was no second sounding, time passed without seeming to be moving at all. He got well west beyond the last horses, and thought that if the remuda hadn't been so worn down Mister

Dixon would have put a nighthawk out, which might have helped.

Beyond sight of camp in a dark world which seemed to have him cut off from everything, he found a worn old boulder and sat beside it to watch and listen. He had been tired, now he was not tired at all. If the Indian found him before he found the Indian . . .

Ordinarily, night-raiders used darkness to stampede livestock, which would then be miles away before pursuit could be undertaken.

If Jeff was right this Indian was not after horses, he was after blood.

The night turned chilly, stars were massed in some mysterious order, the moon was a sickle. By now if that bronco had in mind sneaking up to cut someone's throat, he'd had the time, but one thing was clear, sitting beside the boulder was not going to accomplish anything. He arose slowly, dusted off and started back, moving as stealthily as he had moved getting out here, and again the horses who saw or scented him barely more than turned their heads.

Back in camp he sat down to shed his boots. Nothing had been disturbed, he could hear the snuffling sounds of breathing men, made a stocking-footed round to be sure the tomahawk had not preceded him, and as he was passing the largest lump someone cocked a sixgun.

Jeff froze and waited. A rumbling-deep voice asked just what in the hell he thought he was doing.

Mister Dixon rose up with the cocked pistol. His hair was awry, his discernible features were sleep-puffy and as he awaited a reply he spat aside, finally lowered the hand-gun and growled in disgust as Jeff hunkered down and mentioned the coyote call, his search, and his return.

Mister Dixon gazed owlishly at the cowboy, spat again and eased the hammer down on his sixgun. "I didn't hear no damned coyote," he growled.

Jeff had to admit that maybe it had

really been a coyote, and to also say it probably had been his nerves and imagination, to which the older man's growl turned less hostile as he said, "Get some sleep. If it was an In'ian he'd have tried to run off the horses by now, or sneak into camp and brain someone."

Jeff returned to his blankets, rolled in and lay with both arms under his head gazing upwards. Mister Dixon hadn't been exactly pleased about having his sleep disturbed. Jeff's humiliation didn't bother him very much. He closed his eyes and opened them in what seemed only minutes to the sound of men rigging out their riding stock. Mister Dixon did not say a word as he led off to get the remuda moving again, but Jeff caught him looking mildly disapproving a couple of times.

The horses started out fairly well, tender hooves had been temporarily helped by standing in water. The animals had also eaten and rested.

The day was perfect, not hot and not

cold. The sky was as clear as glass, for half a day the remuda moved ahead without haste, then the sore feet began bothering them so that the drag riders had their hands full.

They were moving over land Jeff was familiar with. Ahead some distance was the entrance to Raton Pass. He rode in pale dust squinting in that direction. Mid-way up there was the last time he and Heber Madden had faced trouble together. For a while he dwelt on other times he and Heber had ridden together. The other riders poked along, unable to travel any faster than the slowest animals they were driving.

They understood the routine very well, whatever they did was accomplished almost mechanically. This was the part of a drive that encouraged boredom.

They rested for an hour with the mouth of Raton Pass clearly visible in the clear air.

Mister Dixon, like his riders, hadn't shaved nor bathed since leaving the Alvarez place. To a stranger they would have looked more like a band of renegades than men doing anything legitimate.

When they pushed ahead again the remuda seemed to crawl, they had the mouth of the pass in sight for hours before they got close to it. Visibility was good despite the dust.

Up there Mister Dixon, riding point, raised an arm. They stopped again, this time so that the remuda would have an opportunity to recover before starting up the pass.

Jeff gazed up there where high bluffs flanked the trail on both sides, and went out among some scrub brush to pee before the drive was resumed because once the remuda was in the pass he would probably have no time for that little chore.

He saw something that almost cut his water off; bare foot horse tracks. He moved among rocks and scrub brush until he was satisfied which way the tracks led, then returned and as the remuda started up the pass, he left

Walt Strong and another man mind the drag as he skirted ahead at a dead walk so as not to upset the horses, got up where Mister Dixon was riding, and told him what he had seen.

The large man rode along looking troubled. He did not speak for a long time. He raised his head to study both sides of the pass, then blew out a ragged breath before speaking.

"That damned fool, what's he expect to accomplish? These horses can't be stampeded, they're too worn down and tender."

Jeff's reply made the large man's unhappy expression deepen. "If he'd wanted to try for the remuda he'd have done it last night. In the dark. If it's the In'ian I think it is, he was the partner of the one called Matador . . . He wants blood."

Mister Dixon slouched along another few yards before speaking again. But first, he ranged a hard look up both sides of the pass they were moving through. "I guess if I was in his boots

240

I'd maybe feel the same way. I'd find me a real good bushwhacking place and wait for the point rider to get within range . . . How does he figure to get clear afterwards?"

"Real easy, Mister Dixon, a gunshot up here sounds like the end of the world. Maybe the remuda can't stampede back down out of here like they done before, but they sure as hell will try, an' in the confusion he'll escape."

"Up them sidehills? He'd better have wings."

Jeff let that remark pass before speaking again. "I could ride up his trail, get above him maybe, or at least find him, while you'n the remuda keep riding."

Mister Dixon did not look very enthusiastic as he spoke again. "Jeff, the point rider'll be out front like a crow settin' on a fence."

Jeff nodded. "I'll find the son of a bitch, but you might let the horses rest for half an hour or so before you get too far on up in here."

The older man eyed his rangeman for a solemn moment, then made a humourless small smile. "Partner, if you don't find him . . . "

Jeff nodded mute agreement; if he failed to find the bushwhacker before the drive got much farther along, Mister Dixon would probably be killed.

The big man nodded. "I'll call a halt up yonder a ways . . . Jeff?"

"I'll do my damndest, Mister Dixon."

"Yeah. Well, good luck."

Jeff eased southward, again riding slowly enough not to upset the remuda. When he got back to the drag he rode stirrup with the laconic tobacco-chewer named Strong, told him what he was going to do, and why, ignored the tall man's look of apprehension and rode back to the place where the ground was wet, picked up barefoot-horse tracks and followed them.

One thing became clear early on. The Indian knew the area up through Raton Pass. He'd probably come up here before daylight, but whether that was true or not, he knew where the thorn-pin bushes were, the largest rocks, and invariably began slanting around them before they appeared.

Jeff understood that. A professional horsethief would have to know his territory, otherwise he would have been found shot or hung long before.

14

At Long Last

THE Indian's route angled closer to the west side of the pass. Jeff guessed he was making toward some upward trail. There were few places a rider could begin the climb. When he saw where the tracks went into a thicket and emerged on the far side, sure enough there was a game trail.

It had two disadvantages, one, it was barely wide enough for a horse to go up it, and if for some reason he might have to turn around, the trail was too narrow for that to be accomplished.

The second disadvantage bothered Jeff the most; along the upward climb from the bottom to the top, he would have no cover and would be visible to anyone watching from above.

He sat a moment eyeing that climb along the front of the barranca and swore under his breath. If the Indian had made that trip in darkness he, and his horse, had to know every inch of it. If he had made the ride about daybreak, possibly he would be far ahead, but if this was not the case, if the bronco was sitting up there watching, he would be able to shoot Jeff any time he chose, Jeff would be like a fly walking up a window, thoroughly exposed.

With knotted innards he urged the thoroughbred up the trail. The animal obeyed as willingly as he always did. If he understood the peril he gave no indication of it.

Fortunately he was long-legged and powerful. He would make the climb more rapidly than most other horses.

Jeff was spared the effects of looking down, he concentrated on looking up. If the bronco was up there he was well concealed, Jeff saw nothing to hold his attention. Except for a few widely separated scrub bushes, the overhead flat country was as swept clean as only country could be where savage winds blew scouring even the soil almost down to bed-rock.

The horses below and their drovers looked small, probably about as they would have looked to a soaring eagle. They were moving up the trail, but at a very slow pace. Riders, particularly the point rider, appeared about doll-size.

Jeff was sweating hard when the big horse made his final lunge and reached the top-out where Jeff swung to the ground so the horse could catch his second wind while his rider studied the countryside.

The tracks went almost due north-ward. They were less discernible up here where topsoil was no more that two or three inches thick, but Jeff walked ahead of his horse for a fair distance before mounting. He was beginning to have a glimmer of the tomahawk's destination — that place up ahead, somewhat past the middle of the pass, where the sniper had fired when Jeff and Heber had been up in here.

He sought cover. What he found was skimpy stands of stunted, wind-twisted underbrush barely high enough to conceal a man. Nowhere nearly tall enough to conceal an animal as tall as the thoroughbred.

The sun also worried this shelterless place. With it came thirst. Jeff left the big horse in a slight depression tied to a wiry bush with little dusty-looking round leaves, scouted ahead darting from meagre shelter to other skimpy safety none of which was really adequate. He had to rely on what he thought the Indian might be doing up ahead somewhere — watching the men and the remuda down below.

It was not the sort of thing a man would ordinarily bet his life on, but here, well on his way to finding the bushwhacker, it was what he had to do without thinking much about the multiplying peril the closer he got to the place where a horse was probably tied or hobbled.

That same nakedness of the plateau above Raton Pass that imperilled Jeff's life with every step, did not favour the ambusher either, except that where he was lying, aside from personal skin-tone and the nondescript, soiled clothing he was wearing which blended perfectly with the sandstone boulders, worn down by years of wind, hid him so well Jeff would probably not have found the man, if he had not found the horse.

The horse was tucked up and head-hung. He had been used without mercy. The climb to the plateau had probably been made on 'bottom' alone. Nor was he a young horse. Even from a fair distance Jeff could see the sunken places above his eyes and the nearly flat chin.

The animal was hobbled in plain sight. The nearest brush was a considerable distance westerly, away from the rim where sandstone boulders, scoured into odd shapes, were closer to the edge overlooking Raton Pass.

Jeff did not exult. The bronco had evidently thought the drovers would not find his trail, which they might not have. He had concentrated all his attention on reaching those sandstone rocks in order to exact his blood vengeance.

With little reason to believe he might be hunted, he had gotten into place before sunrise. As Jeff peered around a thicket at the exhausted horse he remembered something an old Indian had told him one time. If Indians were so good at creeping up on whites, how could it be that the whites were always behind the Indians?

It required time to separate a prone human shape from the sandstone where the man and his hiding place merged. Jeff got north of the indifferent horse, got flat down and went over the land ahead and southward with meticulous care. Even then he might not have seen the Indian if, for some reason, perhaps intuition, the bronco hadn't raised up like a lizard to scan both sides and to the rear.

Jeff was not ready to use his weapon. He held his breath for ten seconds as the narrowed black eyes moved slowly from left to right then back.

A distant shout, so faint it was barely audible, ended the Indian's searching look. As he settled forward among his rocks Jeff had no difficulty outlining him, although if that interlude of uneasiness had not made the Indian move, Jeff might never have found him. Not in time anyway.

Jeff had to assume the shout had been made by one of the men in the pass. He settled close to the ground, moved his weapon slowly forward, saw the bronco suddenly raise his head above his Winchester, peer downward for a long moment, then settle down to snug back the stock and squint through his sights.

The distance was not great. Jeff rested his gunhand on the ground, steadied it with the free hand, cocked the gun and squeezed the trigger before the bushwhacker had more than a second to stiffen when he heard a weapon cocked behind him.

The sound was flat above and only barely audible down below. Jeff watched the Indian as he hauled the hammer back for another shot.

The lethargic horse jumped two feet despite his hobbles. He snorted and began edging away. At least he had that much spirit left.

The Indian had fallen across his Winchester. He was not moving, long, lank black hair riffled slightly as air currents rose up from below. One hand was visible, the other, beneath the bronco on his saddlegun, was not visible.

Jeff arose slowly, leery of a slumped man who had no blood showing. He approached a foot at a time, sixgun extended at full cock, finger curled inside the trigger guard.

When he could, he reached with a

boot to flip the Indian onto his back. The body only half responded, but blood was finally visible. Jeff's slug had caught the man low in the body and had travelled upwards to exit beneath the chin.

Jeff hunkered, wished mightily for a drink of water, did not move for a long time, until he heard more shouting from below, then he went to the edge of the rim and wig-wagged with the bronco's Winchester.

The shouting sounded louder after that as the point rider eased ahead with the remuda. A slight wind swept across the plateau but there was no wind in the canyon.

Jeff tied the Indian belly-down across his own saddle and drove the horse ahead of him back down the hair-raising trail. By the time he reached the pass dust was settling, the remuda was a mile northward. He hoowrahed the Indian horse southward down out of the canyon where someone would eventually see it, and its burden.

The thoroughbred walked northward with the same springy, wide stride he ordinarily used. Jeff talked to him, complimented him, and would spit cotton until late afternoon, close to evening, before he caught up with the drag and Walt Strong handed him a canteen, took it back depleted and rode along through dust without looking at Jeff or saying a word.

Raton Pass was no small cleft, it ran for miles. To those going northward, it was uphill every inch of the way. If the Dixon remuda had been fresh and with sound hooves it would still have been an arduous ordeal. Mister Dixon wanted to reach open country before dark. For that reason tired animals bothered by thirst were pushed where normally they would not have been.

When they finally had most of the canyon behind them the sun was lowering. It would be some time before it left completely which, under normal circumstances would have provided the Dixon remuda with abundant time to cover another four, maybe five miles across fairly open country, but Mister Dixon did not go any farther than a piddling creek which made its crooked path through timber and around some fairly respectable boulders.

Where they halted Mister Dixon left his horse with a rider to be cared for, sprung his legs a few times, watched his head-hung remuda fan out along the little watercourse and when the drag came up, he walked back where Walt Strong was beating dust off with his hat, said something as he passed to which the laconic cowboy nodded, headed over where Jeff Forman was hobbling his animal and said, "I didn't hear any shooting."

Jeff arose with the hobbles in place, tugged loose his latigo with his back to the big man, and replied as he looped the latigo and lifted off the saddle.

"There wasn't none. Just one shot." He looked for a place to up-end the saddle and spread the limp blanket atop it sweat side up, and faced around where Mister Dixon was standing.

"He was at the rim in some big rocks. He was watchin' down below. If that place where he was hiding hadn't tucked back a mite he'd sure as hell have seen me comin' up there. If I'd known any prayers I'd sure have used them on that darned trail."

"Was it the other one?"

Jeff nodded. "Yeah. I come up north of him and in back. He had a target. I don't know whether it was you or someone else. He was concentratin' on what he was doing. He didn't move when I got pretty close behind and shot."

"Did you leave him up there?"

"No. I tied him on his horse, drove it ahead of me down to the canyon and choused it southward. Someone'll find 'em in a day or two."

Mister Dixon stood in thought for a moment before speaking again. "I owe you. When we get home, if you want the job you can be range boss."

Jeff was rolling a cigarette when he

replied. "You don't owe me anythin'."

Someone whistled over near the creek. Mister Dixon walked in that direction as Walt Strong sauntered to where Jeff was lighting up, gazed after the big man for a moment then dryly said, "You goin' to take him up on that foreman's job?"

"No."

The tall man looked quizzically at Jeff. "He ain't hard to work for an' you know the land."

Jeff also turned to look over along the creek where Mister Dixon was conversing with two riders. "He might send me after another bunch of horses." Jeff smiled and Walt Strong smiled back.

They had a camp set up. It was another fire-less camp, not because they did not want firelight to show after dark but because they had nothing that required cooking and nothing to cook in.

Mister Dixon said from here on they would only travel three or four miles a day. No one faulted that; the remuda was in bad shape. If it was allowed to graze along the horses would regain strength, but the only thing hooves worn to the quick required was rest, something Mister Dixon could only provide by driving the remuda very slowly, and when the horses reached their new range, to leave them alone until their hooves grew out again.

The weather held, the days were long, with a drive limited to only a few hours a day there was little for the men to do after they set up camp. They spent time going among the horses, getting acquainted with them. As far as the horses were concerned, they had become accustomed to the men and, excepting a few snorty critters, were leery but not spooky. Mister Dixon was satisfied: he had seen the horses at the time of purchase, but only in a moving band. Close inspection left him satisfied his earlier judgment had been good.

With time on their hands the men

killed game, scouted ahead for places to camp, and in other ways avoided the boredom that invariably was part of a long drive, whether it was cattle or horses being driven.

When they reached the home range, they left the remuda within sight of other Dixon animals and headed for the yard where they cared for their riding animals, trooped to the bunkhouse to settle in again, and to bathe at the big circular tank behind the barn.

Two days later Mister Dixon hunted up Jeff to re-new his offer. Jeff had thought about it on the drive back. His opinion was the same: he did not want to be a foreman. In fact he told Mister Dixon he thought he would ride on even though he knew the fall roundup and drive to the railroad corrals would be getting under way in another six weeks or so.

The large man showed no surprise, nor any annoyance. If there was one thing he had come to accept after a lifetime of cattle ranching it was that rangemen drifted. Not always for reasons they cared to explain, nor for any reason he could understand. It was their nature. In this regard rangemen were rarely predictable.

If someone had told him what Jeff Forman had gone through over the most recent period of time, and for that reason wanted to leave, Mister Dixon would have scoffed. Riders went through things like that as part of their work.

When he was talking to Jeff the subject came up about the big thoroughbred horse; Mister Dixon gave him the horse.

Inadvertently he had come close to discovering why Jeff wanted to leave. He smiled and thanked Mister Dixon. He and the big horse had done more this spring than most rangemen were required to do all season. They had both earned a rest. Summer was at hand, there would be fat trout jumping in mountain lakes, hock-high grass, plenty of shade.

Mister Dixon paid Jeff off, he packed his gatherings and headed out. Heber was settled in, those Alvarez horses had reached their destination, the world was bright and warm, a man needed no more than those things to figure it was time to move on.

He did some figuring; Montana and northern Wyoming would be at their best now; the problem was that they were one hell of a long ride from New Mexico, they did not have long summers. By the time he got up to that country autumn would have set in with bitter winter to follow.

Jeff rode southwest. He knew in that direction if a man rode long enough, he would find country where it rarely snowed, where the sun shone three hundred or more days a year and the roads were paved with gold.

FIGHTING RAMROD
Charles N. Heckelmann

Most men would have cut their losses, but Frazer counted the bullets in his guns and said he'd soak the range in blood before he'd give up another inch of what was his.

LONE GUN
Eric Allen

Smoke Blackbird had been away too long. The Lequires had seized the Blackbird farm, forcing the Indians and settlers off, and no one seemed willing to fight! He had to fight alone.

THE THIRD RIDER
Barry Cord

Mel Rawlins wasn't going to let anything stand in his way. His father was murdered, his two brothers gone. Now Mel rode for vengeance.

ARIZONA DRIFTERS
W. C. Tuttle

When drifting Dutton and Lonnie Steelman decide to become partners they find that they have a common enemy in the formidable Thurston brothers.

TOMBSTONE
Matt Braun

Wells Fargo paid Luke Starbuck to outgun the silver-thieving stagecoach gang at Tombstone. Before long Luke can see the only thing bearing fruit in this eldorado will be the gallows tree.

HIGH BORDER RIDERS
Lee Floren

Buckshot McKee and Tortilla Joe cut the trail of a border tough who was running Mexican beef into Texas. They stopped the smuggler in his tracks.

BRETT RANDALL, GAMBLER
E. B. Mann

Larry Day had the choice of running away from the law or of assuming a dead man's place. No matter what he decided he was bound to end up dead.

THE GUNSHARP
William R. Cox

The Eggerleys weren't very smart. They trained their sights on Will Carney and Arizona's biggest blood bath began.

THE DEPUTY OF SAN RIANO
Lawrence A. Keating and
Al. P. Nelson

When a man fell dead from his horse, Ed Grant was spotted riding away from the scene. The deputy sheriff rode out after him and came up against everything from gunfire to dynamite.

FARGO: MASSACRE RIVER
John Benteen

The ambushers up ahead had now blocked the road. Fargo's convoy was a jumble, a perfect target for the insurgents' weapons!

SUNDANCE: DEATH IN THE LAVA
John Benteen

The Modoc's captured the wagon train and its cargo of gold. But now the halfbreed they called Sundance was going after it . . .

HARSH RECKONING
Phil Ketchum

Five years of keeping himself alive in a brutal prison had made Brand tough and careless about who he gunned down . . .

FARGO: PANAMA GOLD
John Benteen

With foreign money behind him, Buckner was going to destroy the Panama Canal before it could be completed. Fargo's job was to stop Buckner.

FARGO:
THE SHARPSHOOTERS
John Benteen

The Canfield clan, thirty strong were raising hell in Texas. Fargo was tough enough to hold his own against the whole clan.

PISTOL LAW
Paul Evan Lehman

Lance Jones came back to Mustang for just one thing — revenge! Revenge on the people who had him thrown in jail.